HARD COPY

By Richard Ayres

Published by New Generation Publishing in 2021

Copyright © Richard Ayres 2021

First Edition

ISBN 978-1-80031-148-0

www.newgeneration-publishing.com

 New Generation Publishing

Acknowledgements

The author wishes to thank the following for the encouragement and constructive criticism they gave while I was writing this novel –

Paul, David, Jehane, Angie, Eddie, Ralph, Judith, Catherine, Francis, Martin

PART ONE – WINTER

Chapter 1

Doreen and Eileen, both widowed and in their late 70s, had moved into Barnes Avenue within a few weeks of each other in the 1960s. It had then been part of a council estate, but in common with most other tenants, they had exercised the right bestowed on them by Mrs Thatcher in 1980 to buy their homes at a large discount. Many of the houses had since been sold on, and the estate was no longer the close-knit community they remembered.

The joys and agonies of child-rearing had brought them close together. Their closeness was literal as well as metaphorical, for they were near neighbours. Only one house separated them, the other half of the semi-detached in which Doreen lived. This was occupied by a Jeremy and Helen Johnson. But despite twenty-five years having passed since the Johnsons had moved in, the couple were still largely a mystery to Doreen and Eileen.

It was the Johnsons they were about to discuss as they sat in Eileen's small front room. Their daily meetings usually took place in the afternoon, but earlier that morning, Doreen has been visited by her grandson Kevin, who'd told her something that she thought Eileen ought to know immediately.

'Come on then, Doreen,' said Eileen, tea having been poured and chocolate biscuits dispensed, 'spill the beans about your Kevin.'

'Well, you know our Kev's a student at the college doing his A levels? He called round early today with a recipe book I'd left at his mum's. I said I hoped it wouldn't make him late for his lectures, but he said it didn't matter because the lecturer was – well, I won't say the word he used; you know what teenagers' language is like.'

'I can imagine. Go on.'

'Apparently this lecturer – he teaches English – is a part-timer, and Kev said it was a bloody good job because all the students hate him. Apparently, he's a miserable, stuck-up ... well, *bastard* was the word Kev used. Kev and his mates call him Jeremiah. I asked him what the fellow's real name was.' She took a sip of tea.

'Get on with it, Doreen!'

'His name's Jeremy Johnson!' Doreen took a triumphant swig of tea and awaited her friend's reaction.

In fact, Eileen had already guessed that but hadn't liked to spoil her friend's story. She'd noticed recently that Doreen's memory wasn't what it once was, and she'd obviously forgotten that Jeremy Johnson used to teach English at the local college. But two things *had* surprised Eileen: one, she thought he no longer worked there, and two, Johnson had never struck her as someone who could really be described as a bastard.

'Well, it's a surprise, Doreen, because the last we heard, he resigned from that job ages ago.'

Doreen frowned in puzzlement, then raised her arm to smack her forehead, spilling some of her tea in the process. Then she shook her head from side to side, muttering to herself, *Of course he did! Of course!* before saying, 'Oh, what's happening to my brain, Eileen?'

'Oh, don't worry, dear, we all forget things at our age; I certainly do. In any case, it was me who Helen told about her Jeremy resigning, so that's probably why it stuck in my mind. That was back in the days when Helen used to talk to us a bit.'

The two friends then began discussing the Johnsons, Eileen frequently prompting Doreen by such remarks as *Do you remember when?* and Doreen occasionally responding with memories of her own. Like all elderly people, they took comfort in the accord resulting from shared experiences stretching back half a lifetime, with any disagreements they might once have had having been almost forgotten.

They agreed that the Johnsons had struck them as a strange couple from the time they'd first moved in. They'd had a baby girl called Jane, and Helen Johnson had begun exchanging 'hellos' with Eileen and Doreen on the occasions she'd met them while out wheeling the child in her pram. But other than that, she'd said nothing; indeed, she'd seemed very withdrawn, and it was only after the baby became a toddler that, prompted by Eileen and Doreen cooing over her, she'd begun talking to them. She'd sounded quite posh. But she'd hardly ever mentioned her husband beyond telling them he was an English lecturer at the local F.E. college. They'd never seen Jeremy with the child; indeed, they'd seen little of him at all except sometimes when he left the house for work or when he returned home in the evening. On those occasions, he'd muttered a *good morning* or *good evening* but had barely glanced at them. They'd been unable to decide whether he was shy or snooty. They'd agreed he was a nondescript fellow, average height, a bit on the porky side, mousy hair, not really ugly, but certainly not handsome because of his big nose and ears.

'So when was it you reckon he gave up his full-time job at the college?' asked Doreen.

'Oh, I can remember that quite clearly. It was when young Jane started at primary school. She'd have been five then, of course. The reason it's so clear in my mind is because Helen began working at the same school the very same day Jane started. She was a part-time teaching assistant, whatever that is. She still is, as far as I know. She told me that now she was earning money, Jeremy was going to give up his job and concentrate on writing.'

'Oy yes, I remember now! But I never really got what that meant.'

'I asked Helen, remember? And she said he was writing … oh, what did she call it? Literary fiction! That was it! But I never really understood what that was. I kept meaning to ask her, but after she started work we didn't get to see her so much, did we? Even in the school holidays.'

At this point Doreen, at last, felt able to make a longer contribution to the discussion, for she had the advantage of sharing a party-wall with the Johnsons and had sometimes heard what went on in their house. She reminded Eileen (though Eileen didn't need reminding) that the couple used to argue a lot and that she'd often heard Helen screaming at her daughter, which often resulted in tears. Sometimes she thought she'd heard Helen crying as well. Doreen was also able to look over into the Johnsons' back garden, which was a mess: she'd never seen Johnson working in it, and the only time she'd seen Helen sitting out in it was when her husband wasn't at home.

'He was out of the house an awful lot, Eileen. If he didn't have a job, where d'you think he used to go? D'you reckon he had a fancy piece on the side somewhere?'

'Johnson? No! He wasn't exactly God's gift to women, was he? Mind you, Helen wasn't at all pretty. No, I think he spent a lot of time down in the library. When I was out shopping I used to see him sometimes, going in and out of the place. Doing his writing, I suppose.'

'I wonder why he's gone back to teaching at the college?'

'Who knows? And we'll never know now, will we, not since Helen's stopped talking to us.'

'And the other thing I'd like to know is what happened to young Jane. We hardly ever saw her when she was a teenager at school, did we?'

'No, and when she left school, she left home as well, and her only sixteen! Something weird was going on there. Don't you remember I asked Helen where she'd gone? She just ran into the house. It was after that she stopped talking to me altogether.'

Doreen glanced at her watch. 'Oh, Eileen, it's nearly one o'clock! I'd better be off. Lucy's coming round for a bite to eat soon.'

The two exchanged affectionate farewells. Recently, they'd begun hugging each other on meeting and parting, something they'd never done as young women. Was this because they were aware that their advancing years would soon result in their final parting? Or was it because they'd become accustomed to seeing young people exchanging public hugs and kisses and that these 21st century customs had rubbed off on them? This was something that fascinated Eileen but was not something she felt able to discuss with Doreen, who these days only seemed to enjoy gossiping about other people.

Eileen escorted Doreen to the front door and stood there to give her a parting wave before hurrying back indoors to mop up the tea that Doreen had spilt on her new carpet. Doreen, walking to her house, hunched against the incessant wind and rain, and still thinking about their conversation, was unaware of the man walking towards her until she bumped into him.

'I beg your pardon,' was muttered at her, and she was taken aback to find it was Jeremy Johnson. The coincidence amazed her. She'd just been talking about him but hadn't seen him for weeks. It was almost as though he'd known that he was in her thoughts and had decided to invade them.

'Oh, my fault, Mr Johnson.'

He made to walk on, but Doreen decided to take advantage of the coincidental encounter.

'Oh, Mr Johnson, d'you mind me asking you something?'

He stopped and faced her. 'What's that, then, Mrs Ellis? I've got things to do. I'm afraid I can't give you long.'

'It's just that I think you might know my grandson. Kevin Daltry's his name, and he's in your English class at the college.'

'I teach a large number of students on a variety of courses. I'm sorry, but I can't remember all their names. Now, if you'll excuse me – '

'It's just that I didn't know you'd gone back to teaching at the college until Kevin – '

'I'm sorry, I really must get on now. Goodbye, Mrs Ellis.'

He turned away. Doreen was rather offended by his attitude and resolved to tell Kevin and his mum about the conversation.

*

Jeremy was annoyed when he entered his house. So much so that he failed to register the mess left behind by Helen in her hurry to get to work, something that usually depressed him.

It was that Mrs Ellis from next door who had annoyed him, bloody inquisitive woman. Yes, he knew Kevin Daltry only too well, one of those idiots who obviously took pleasure in disrupting his lectures by constantly interrupting to ask inane questions, questions which would eventually be answered if only they'd listen attentively to his lectures which were delivered with the eloquence of which he was proud.

Surrendering to his anger, he hurled his briefcase across the kitchen. It skidded across the table, dislodging unwashed crockery, an uneaten piece of toast and an open packet of cereals onto the floor, which itself bore all the hallmarks of a surface that hadn't been cleaned for weeks. Jeremy was now only too aware of the squalor of his surroundings.

But his anger was not directed at Helen, but at Mrs Ellis who, by mentioning the college, had re-awakened all the disappointments and frustrations that had plagued his life ever since he'd left university thirty years ago with a First Class Honours degree in English Literature

It had been his intention to stay on at university to study for a master's degree, with the idea of following this with a PhD and then a career in academia. But then Helen, a fellow student, had pronounced herself pregnant following the one-night stand they'd had (in fact, it had been his first-ever stand) at a party held to celebrate the end of finals. If that were not bad enough, she'd refused to get an abortion because she and her parents were devout Christians. At their insistence, and himself being conscience-stricken, he'd had no alternative but to marry her.

With that, his dream of a career in academia had evaporated. He'd needed to get a job to support a wife and child. Teaching had been his only option. In the end, he'd had to settle for a junior lecturer's post in an F.E. college in Watford of all places and to live in a small semi in what had once been a council estate. At least his father had left him enough money to buy it outright. He'd disliked his job at the college, and since he'd had to return there to teach as a mere part-timer, he loathed it.

No, he must try not to think of all that. He must get on with what he'd been intending to do before that damned Mrs Ellis had reminded him of all that had gone before. He found he was sitting at the kitchen table, and he had no idea how long he'd been there. Should he clear up the mess? No, surely Helen ought to have washed up her breakfast things. After all, she no longer had a rebellious teenager to contend with.

He picked up his briefcase and carried it up to the poky bedroom, which he'd commandeered as his study after Jane left. As he sat at the computer, his mood began to lighten, for he was engaged on a project which he hoped might eventually lead to the success he knew he deserved.

He hadn't told Helen anything about it. As far as she was concerned, he spent his time up here writing his novel and preparing lectures.

Chapter 2

Jeremy's computer was over ten years old, and on its last legs. He'd had to buy it on hire-purchase, though he'd told Helen he had enough money put by to purchase it outright.

'Then why,' she'd said, 'didn't you buy something we really need, like a new vacuum cleaner or even a dishwasher? Look, I'm the main breadwinner now, aren't I? You might at least consider buying something to help me with the housework. After all, you don't help me with it, do you?'

'No, I'm sorry about that,' he'd said. 'It's just that I'm so tied up with this novel and – '

'You need to concentrate; I know, so you keep telling me. Put another record on, can't you?'

'Helen, I've been wondering; if you want more money, well, had you thought about getting a job in the school holidays? There must be plenty of jobs going in supermarkets and – '

He hadn't been allowed to explain. She'd charged out of the room and slammed the door behind her.

In fact, Jeremy's main motivation for suggesting she get a holiday job had been to ensure she kept busy. During the holidays, she always became depressed and tearful, probably because, with nothing else to occupy her mind, she relapsed into thinking about Jane. She still did, after all these years. And so did he.

Jeremy couldn't understand Helen's assertion that he should spend time doing housework. Surely she should realise that he needed long periods of time alone and undisturbed in order to concentrate on producing a work that would be of interest to publishers of literary fiction?

He turned on the computer. It always took an age to come to life, and he dreaded the inevitable day when it would expire. At least he had no work-in-progress installed on it.

He'd had no time to consider his next novel since having to return to work part-time at that bloody F.E. college four years ago. But for his new project, he relied on it completely.

He was impatient for the machine to turn on, for he knew that two unread emails awaited him. He'd checked before leaving for work. He assumed they'd contain the attachments he'd been waiting for, those he needed to work on in order to obtain the next meagre instalments of his earnings.

At last! Life in the old PC yet! He tapped on his second Gmail account, and yes, the two emails contained attachments. The messages were from Stephanie Bridges and Colonel Collinson, both of whom knew Jeremy as Albert Rennie, the name which he'd adopted for his business. He'd also opened a second bank account under the name Rennie Literary Services.

Stephanie's email read: *Hi Albert, here's my chapter 6. Please confirm you've received it.* He opened her attachment – yes, five pages of writing that he knew would verge on chick-lit.

Collinson's email read: *Mr Rennie, herewith the next instalment of my autobiography. I hope you can return it to me sooner than you usually do and with fewer unnecessary amendments.* He knew it would comprise about ten pages of exposition that would be better described as a diary, something which, as with Stephanie Bridges' effort, would require not just proofreading but careful copy-editing. Not that he minded that. He could charge more for editing.

The front door slammed. Oh God, she was home already. He was unable to work when she was at home, even though she rarely interrupted him when he was in his study. Just being aware of her presence in the house was a distraction. It had been when he was writing his novels, and it was still the case now he was engaged on his new project.

Sighing, he turned off the computer and went out onto the landing, just in time to hear, 'Oh, for heaven's sake,

Jeremy, you might at least have made an attempt to clear up the mess in the kitchen.'

He went downstairs, steeling himself for the inevitable debate. He knew that afterwards, he'd be unable to settle to work, so he decided to attend a meeting of the local writers group that evening.

*

The Rebel Writers Group met fortnightly in the small back room of the *Saracen's Head*, a pub in one of the less salubrious Watford suburbs. Jeremy's attendance at the meetings was becoming ever less frequent because he knew he was getting little from them.

One of the group members, Ralph, whom Jeremy respected, had told him about the group's Facebook page. On it, the chairman, one Claud Almond, proclaimed that the meetings were intended only for those who were serious about becoming published authors. But it was only after a few weeks that new members came to realise that Claud Almond had his own rigid opinions about what was publishable, and if their work didn't fit his bill, it was subject to carping criticism not only from him but from his acolytes in the group of which there were several.

Most members suffering these indignities soon left, to be replaced by a new cohort of innocents. Only those who wrote fantasy, horror or action novels were consistent attendees. Jeremy had often considered leaving the group himself. What was he, a man who by rights should be a member of the elite academic literati, doing by exposing his talents to an uncomprehending bunch of semi-literates? This was a question he often asked himself, but he was usually reluctant to admit the truth, that he was lonely. Attempting to write novels had resulted in even more isolation.

He was late arriving at the meeting. It was a half-hour walk to the pub, and it had started raining just after he'd set off. Soaked, he was depressed, still thinking about his disagreement with Helen, and in no mood to tolerate Almond's disparaging comments. He entered the pub, went straight to the gents – something he was finding he was having to do with increasing frequency – then purchased a half-pint of cider and pushed open the door leading to the poky back room. Almond was sitting, his posture radiating self-importance, at the head of the table.

'Ah, so we have the pleasure of the company of Mr Johnson this evening!' he said. 'Well, we'll count ourselves lucky that you've decided to grace us with your presence, for as you see, there are fewer of us here than usual. Do you have something to read to us, Jeremy? I'm sure we're all waiting for your offering with bated breath.' His fan-club gathered near him at the top of the table sniggered.

Jeremy managed to retain his composure, though he was tempted to point out that Almond had ended his last sentence with a cliché. He confirmed that he had brought something to read and took his usual seat at the far end of the table from Almond. There were indeed fewer members present than when he'd last attended, and he wondered if Judith, David and Ralph, the only people whose writing he'd enjoyed, had left the group, probably despairing that they would ever receive constructive observations. But at least that had resulted in the room being less crowded, though it was still insufferably hot, and he was not spared the body odour of the wizened Olive Grimley who was sitting next to him.

'So,' said Almond. Jeremy was always irritated by those who began a remark with a proclamatory 'So'. 'I suggest we start by listening to Jeremy's contribution before the break. I'm sure we'll all welcome the chance to get another drink after we've heard it.' More sniggers from the Almond-end of the table.

Jeremy pulled the typewritten A4 sheets from his briefcase, stood up – it was a requirement that one stood to read – cleared his throat and began. He almost knew the piece by heart, despite having written it more than ten years before. It was a chapter from his first, unpublished, novel.

Both the novels he'd written remained unpublished, despite his having sent them to almost every reputable publisher in the country. He'd tried to find an agent to act for him, but their responses, though sometimes complimentary, had indicated that his work was unlikely to attract a wide readership and that on this occasion, they regretted that they'd be unable to act on his behalf. He hadn't considered self-publishing because he couldn't afford the exorbitant charges this would involve, and in any case, to self-publish was to admit failure.

He completed his reading and sat down. Almond usually began the discussion following a reading, but on this occasion, he first invited comments from those sitting near him. There were many comments:

'When are we going to get some action?'

'That character wouldn't do that, would she?'

'Your descriptions are far too long!'

'Why do you use all those backstories? They slow down the plot.'

'Most readers would give up on this book after about four chapters.'

'Why don't you introduce some fantasy or horror, or even sex?'

'Why do you use all those long words that nobody's ever heard of? You need a dictionary to understand what you're trying to say.'

These were the suggestions hurled at Jeremy. He didn't respond to them, preferring to remain silent until after Almond had delivered his concluding remarks.

'Well,' said Almond, smirking, 'I don't think there's anything I need to add. Everything's been said that I think needed to be said. Is there anything you'd like to say in response, Jeremy?'

Jeremy knew he must remain cool and composed, having just decided that he was going to make a farewell statement. He stood up and looked round the table, making eye contact with each of those to whom his remarks would be aimed.

'First of all, Claud, I'd like to repeat an observation I made soon after I began attending these meetings, which was that if each of us were to distribute to the group in advance a hard copy of what we are to read, then comments could be made about the strengths and weaknesses of each person's style, grammar, punctuation and syntax. It is difficult to make instant judgements about these from simply listening to what is read out.'

'So how come audiobooks are becoming so popular, eh, Jeremy?'

'I think you're making my point for me, Claud. Audiobooks are popular precisely because they make no demands on the listener, as is also the case with readers of much best-selling fiction. Surely the purpose of a writers' group such as this should be for us to learn from each other how to hone our writing skills by engaging in mutual literary criticism?'

'Literary criticism? Well, one of the many things I've learned from running a publishing company is that literary criticism is a matter of personal taste.'

Jeremy smiled. Almond's statement had provided him with a perfect introduction to his final remark.

'In many ways you are right, Claud. But the problem is that you, and others here in your inner circle, are totally devoid of any literary taste whatsoever. To put it simply, and I'm aware that simplicity is something you worship, you are all tasteless. I bid you goodnight.'

He picked up his briefcase and made for the door. There was silence in the room, but he heard Olive Grimley break it.

'Who does he think he is, a bloody university lecturer?'

The sense of elation that Jeremy felt after he'd left the room was short-lived. It was still raining hard outside, and he had a half-hour walk to get home to a no-doubt silent Helen. They had long ceased to give each other comfort. Now, he was faced tomorrow with another morning trying to teach those morons at the college. And still, after twenty years, he'd not had a novel published.

Chapter 3

Although the room was graced with the title College Refectory, it was the sole preserve of students. Lecturers used to frequent it, but they now had their own refreshment facilities. The refectory, badly in need of redecoration, now housed battered Formica tables, littered at break-time with empty bottles, cans, and plastic cups. These would not be cleared away until just before lunch when heated-up frozen meals would take their place. The women at the serving hatch resented their role as dispensers of fodder to ill-mannered louts who couldn't be bothered to clear up after themselves and envied their fortunate colleagues who worked in the staff coffee bar and dining room.

Kevin Daltry was dithering in front of the self-service machine. He couldn't decide whether to have a Pepsi or an apple juice.

'Get a fuckin' move on!' shouted Joe. 'We 'ent got all day! Jeremiah's lecture starts in ten minutes, dunnit?'

Joe was sitting with the others at a nearby table. Kevin chose a Pepsi and carried it over to join his mates, all students on the GCE A Level English course. He sat down amongst them.

'Come on then, Kev,' said Andy, 'what is it you got to tell us about Jeremiah?'

Kevin had sent them all a WhatsApp message the previous evening in which he'd said that his grandmother and mother had told him things about Jeremy Johnson which he thought they could use to get at him.

'Well, my gran lives next door to Jeremiah. He and his missus had a kid, a girl, and Gran reckons she heard the kid being knocked about – she used to hear her screaming.'

'Fuckin' hell,' said Joe.

'That's not all. She reckons she heard the girl being caned upstairs in her bedroom when she was a teenager.'

'That's appalling!' said Carol. She lifted her can of Diet Coke and took a delicate sip from it.

'Anyway,' Kevin continued. 'Me gran and me mum never saw anything of Jane after she left school. They reckon she ran away from home.'

'So how do you think we can use this information, Kev?' This from Terry, one of the more serious in the group.

'Dunno. Thought you lot might have some ideas.'

'Why don't yer just come right out and ask the minger if it's true, Kev?' said Joe. Joe was always up for a bit of bother.

'But he'd never let me speak, would he? Like, he never lets any of us interrupt him, does he?'

'Well,' said Andy, 'how about asking him before he starts his lecture?'

'Oh, come on, Andy. He'd shut me up, and if I tried to carry on talking, he'd chuck me out, wouldn't he?'

'Well, why not wait till he's finished his lecture?' ventured Terry. 'He always keeps us sitting there till he's ready to leave.'

'Oh yeah. And I bet as soon as I spoke, he'd walk straight out.'

'What about you, Carol?' said Andy. 'He might let *you* speak. He does sometimes, doesn't he?'

'Yeah, and we all know why that is, don't we?' said Joe. 'It's because the dirty old minger fancies yer. You've said yerself how he stares at yer tits.'

'Yes, he's a sexist bastard just like you, Joe,' said Carol. 'Anyway, why should I carry the can for you lot?'

'Hang on a bit, Carol,' said Kevin. 'I reckon Joe might be on to something. I think he lets you interrupt him sometimes because … well, because he knows you're clever, I suppose.'

Kevin was in awe of Carol. She seemed so much older in her ways than the rest of the group. She took her studies seriously, read all the set books and many more besides. This was obvious from some of the things she'd managed to say to Jeremiah in his lectures. She was mature in other ways, as well. Unlike the other girls at the college, she dressed like a smart young woman; no teenage ripped jeans or micro-skirts or crop-tops for her. She was what his dad would call a classy piece. Kevin knew she was way beyond his reach.

'Well, thank you, Kev,' she said. 'Actually, I do have an idea of a way we might get him to listen to us. You realise what he'll be lecturing about today?'

'It'll be crap, that's for sure,' said Joe.

Everybody laughed. Joe often said that English Literature was a pain in the arse, airy-fairy bullshit which wouldn't qualify anyone for a proper job and that he was thinking of giving it up so he could concentrate on economics and sociology. Carol had told him he'd be doing them all a favour if he did.

'It's going to be about *Jane Eyre*, isn't it?' said Terry.

'Yes, and we're supposed to have finished reading it by now, if you remember,' said Carol. 'Hasn't it occurred to you that some of the themes and motifs in the novel have similarities to what Kevin's told us about Jeremiah's daughter?'

The group stared at her blank-faced. When she used words like 'themes' and 'motifs' they were reminded of her cleverness, and, in any case, few of them had read beyond the first few chapters of Brontë's novel, so had no idea what she was talking about.

Then something occurred to Kevin. 'Oh, d'you mean that Jane has the same name as Jeremiah's daughter?'

'No, that's just a coincidence, Kevin.'

'Well, I still don't get how the book'll help us get at him.'

'I haven't time to explain now, it's eleven; we'd better get to his session.'

She led the way towards the lecture room. Kevin followed close behind her, still with no idea what she was going to say. Even as he was wondering about this, he was turned on by the way she was swinging her hips.

The group entered the lecture room to find four other students already seated. There were only nine in the class; it had started out having fourteen.

Jeremy was standing erect behind his desk at the front, his hands clasping his jacket lapels. He waited until the latecomers were seated, then pronounced, 'Punctuality is the politeness of princes. Those who have belatedly arrived would do well to remember this.'

'Wanker,' Kevin heard Joe mutter.

'On the assumption that you have all completed reading *Jane Eyre*,' Jeremy began, 'I shall today be considering the era in which the story is set. I shall be paying particular attention to the social mores of the early 19th century in the context of the various social groups which are portrayed. It is only when this is understood that the motivations and actions of the various characters can be fully appreciated, and I shall be examining the skill, or otherwise, with which Charlotte Brontë handles this.'

He rarely referred to the lecture notes on the desk in front of him. As he spoke, he walked slowly back and forth in front of the class, his hands never leaving his jacket lapels. His lecture was delivered in a monotone, there was no hint of humour in its content, and he never looked at his students, his gaze directed towards something above their heads.

As his lecture proceeded, his students' attention began to wander. Only a few bothered to take notes.

Kevin lapsed into the thoughts that always came to him when Johnson was in full flow. He was fantasising about Carol, who was sitting in front of him.

'… and, of course, the mores of English society in the early 19th century,' Jeremiah was intoning, 'were such that such treatment of children was considered quite acceptable and – '

'Excuse me, Mr Johnson, may I ask a question?'

Jeremy looked startled, then annoyed. His hands dropped from his jacket lapels, he stopped walking about, and his gaze left the middle distance to alight on Carol. His expression softened on seeing her.

'Very well, Miss Harvey, as we're nearing the end of the lecture, I will make an exception and allow your interruption. What is it you want to ask?'

'Well, you said that the way Jane Eyre was treated was acceptable at the time. She was beaten by Mrs Reed, and Mr Brocklehurst made her stand on a stool for hours without food, didn't he?'

'Yes. Your point being?'

'Well, it was physical abuse of a child, wasn't it? But that didn't just take place in the 19th century, did it? It still happens. I'm sure some children still run away because their parents ill-treat them.'

Awesome! thought Kevin. Carol had really made her point.

She was still standing, awaiting a reply from Jeremy. None came. It was the first time the class had seen him speechless. After nearly a minute during which the room was totally silent, he spoke.

'Miss Harvey, I fail to see what relevance your observation has to the study of a classic of 19th century English literature. This lecture is now concluded'.

With that, he picked up his briefcase and left the room.

*

Jeremy would have liked to have gone home to lose himself in his copy-editing, but he had another lecture to deliver in an hour to a 2nd year A Level class. There was no alternative but to go to the main staffroom. As a part-timer, he wasn't entitled to a desk in the general studies workroom.

The staffroom was not a place in which he felt at ease; it was always full of engineering, catering, business studies and other vocational lecturers with whom he had little in common, but he could do with a coffee while he waited for his next class. But first, he must visit the toilet.

Relieved, and waiting in the queue to be served coffee, he mulled over what Carol Harvey had said. She was an intelligent young woman, mature for her years, and he had often wondered why she'd chosen to attend an F.E. college, a depository for second-raters, rather than stay on in the local school 6th form. He'd checked her records and had found she'd passed all her GCSEs with top grades. He sometimes allowed her to interrupt his lectures to ask questions because they were always astute and pertinent.

But on this occasion, her interruption hadn't taken the form of a question. It was a statement about contemporary physical abuse of children. Why? Was it perhaps because she was also studying sociology? Or had she intended launching into a feminist diatribe, given that the victim of the abuse in Bronte's novel was a young female? Yes, that was probably it. Carol Harvey was of the generation of young women who saw everything through the lens of perceived female subjugation, though he'd noticed that this didn't prevent her from flaunting her assets on occasions when she wanted attention.

'Hey, darling, it's your turn to be served!' A hand touched his elbow.

He started, and turned to see a fat woman grinning at him. He recognised her as one of the lecturers from the Health and Beauty department who always frequented, noisily, the same corner of the staffroom.

'Miles away then, weren't you!'

'Yes. I'm sorry.'

He asked the woman at the counter for a cup of black coffee, and once served, he took it to one of the few tables which were unoccupied.

He wasn't alone for long. Three young men whom he recognised as sports studies lecturers took up the seats at his table. Sports studies! Such a discipline hadn't existed when he'd been a full-timer at the college. He'd first assumed it was a grandiose name for what used to be the P.E. Department but had recently learned that one could read for a degree in sports studies at several of the newer universities and that one such course even had a David Beckham module. Jeremy was despairing of what was happening to education.

His thoughts were interrupted on hearing one of those at his table address his colleague as Kevin. Instantly, he was taken back to what had happened in his lecture and the fact that Kevin Daltry was a member of the class and was one of Carol Harvey's crowd. Then, the realisation hit him. Daltry was the grandson of Mrs Ellis next door, and she knew he was in his class and … no! Surely not? What did that woman know about Jane? Would she have told Kevin Daltry? Had Daltry told Carol Harvey whatever it was he'd discovered about Jane?

No. He must be rational. That unlikely scenario was of the kind to be found in poorly contrived novels, similar to the sort of thing that Stephanie Bridges was writing. And yes, he should concentrate on proofreading and copy-editing her manuscript. It gave him far more satisfaction than lecturing to teenagers who showed little interest in the knowledge he had to impart.

'Oh, Jeremy. I thought you might be in here.'

It was Harold Fletcher, Jeremy's faculty head.

'Hello, Harold.'

'Jeremy, would you come to my office after your next lecture? There's something we need to discuss.'

Jeremy groaned. Was there no getting away from this bloody place?

Chapter 4

Harold Fletcher was waiting for Jeremy to arrive. The bugger was taking his time. Was he trying to make a point, Harold wondered? He sometimes thought that Jeremy did not have the respect for him that his status as faculty head merited, probably because they'd been junior lecturers together back in the early 90s when Harold was teaching history.

Harold had never been friendly with him. Jeremy had seemed reluctant to join in work-room banter. Some in the faculty said he was shy, others that he was an intellectual snob. Indeed, Harold had heard him make the occasional disparaging remark about other disciplines. He'd once told the geography lecturer that his subject was purely descriptive and was totally devoid of concepts.

But the year after Harold had arrived, Jeremy had resigned, and Harold had no chance to get to know him better. Harold found it strange that nobody in the faculty, not even Jim Ellison, his English colleague, had known if he'd obtained another post elsewhere, and after Jim retired, Jeremy had become a fading memory.

Harold still felt lucky to have possessed organisational abilities – no, managerial, one had to call them now. Within four years of his appointment, he'd been promoted to be a senior lecturer, and a few years after that, deputy head of faculty. On the retirement of his boss, he'd applied for and obtained the faculty head's post and had inherited the poky office in which he was now sitting uncomfortably on his upright chair.

He'd left his door ajar, and Jeremy entered without having knocked.

'Ah, Jeremy, thanks for coming. Take a seat.'

Jeremy sat down on the chair opposite Harold's desk. Harold picked up his own chair and positioned it so he was seated next to Jeremy. How should he begin what was going to be a difficult interview? It was hard to think of any preliminary chat that might soften the blow of the things that needed to be said.

'How are things with you, Jeremy? I rarely get time to talk to you these days. Remind me; how long is it that you've been back here with us as a part-timer?'

'I'm well enough. This is my fourth year here.'

This was said without his making eye-contact. He rarely did. Some said this an indication of shyness, others of shiftiness. Now that he was sitting at close quarters, Harold noticed that his large nose had open pores and was peppered with red blotches. He noticed also that his jacket was shabby, and his shirt looked none too clean. His hair could do with a wash as well.

'Ah yes, of course. Time flies, doesn't it? I'm sorry we could only find you a part-time post, but you know how it was, and still is, in F.E. Continual spending cuts. When lecturers leave, we can often only afford to replace them with part-timers.'

'Yes, so you said when you interviewed me.'

In fact, there had been only one other applicant for the post. Jeremy had been the most experienced, so Harold had appointed him, albeit with some reservations. On his application form, he'd provided no references because he claimed to have been self-employed as an author since leaving his full-time post at the college. Harold's reservations about Jeremy's suitability for the job had increased over the years he'd been teaching part-time.

'Jeremy, the reason I've asked you in for a chat is that I'm concerned about the high drop-out rate from your first-year A Level Class. We're only halfway through the spring term, and the numbers have dropped from fourteen to nine. Do you have any idea why that should be?'

'Probably because those who dropped out had realised they weren't intelligent enough to stand any chance of success in their examinations.' This was said quietly without any hint of defensiveness. He was still not making eye-contact.

'But they haven't given up any of their other subjects.'

'And what are those subjects?'

'Geography, history, sociology and economics, as far as I can remember.'

'Well, all they need to do to succeed in those is to learn the facts and regurgitate them in the examinations. The study of English literature requires much more than that, you see – '

'Just hang on a minute, Jeremy. This is about more than just your high drop-out rates.'

For the first time since he'd been in the room, Johnson glanced at him, then looked away hurriedly. Harold noticed his hands were clenched.

'Jeremy, no students have dropped out of your second-year class. Have you any idea why this should be?'

'Presumably by the time they reach the second-year they've come to realise –'

'I'll tell you why. It's because you take them for only one of their five sessions each week. Marion takes the other sessions, and apparently much of her time is taken up discussing with them the things you should have covered. And no, it wasn't Marion who told me this. The information came to me in letters I've received from some parents, and –'

'Which parents?'

'You must realise I can't divulge that, Jeremy. The correspondence is confidential.'

Johnson half rose from his seat, then slumped back. His expression was hard to fathom. Harold knew it would be best to get straight to the point in the hope that he would realise what was best for him and resign, but he felt a measure of sympathy for him. Did the fellow have any other source of income? The state of his clothing indicated otherwise. Looking at him, he seemed now to be devoid of the arrogance which characterised his dealings with his students and colleagues. Harold decided it would be best to start by trying to engage in counselling.

'When you applied for your part-time post, Jeremy, you said on your application form that you were a self-employed author. Are you still writing? Have you had any books published?'

'I have several works in progress.'

'So you don't have any income from book sales?'

'What has this to do with the matter we're discussing?'

'I'm just interested in how you earn a living, apart from teaching here, of course.'

'I'm not sure that's any concern of yours, but if you must know, I have a business which proof-reads and copy-edits manuscripts.'

'Oh. Interesting. How have you managed to build up the business?'

'I assume you've heard of LinkedIn?'

'Yes, it's one of those social media things on the internet, isn't it?'

Johnson smiled, leaned back in his chair, and grasped the lapels of his jacket. 'Hardly. It's a professional networking system which helps career development. On it, one can enhance one's professional profile. I use it to advertise my skills and offer my services to people who have need of them. It is invaluable in – '

'Hang on a minute, Jeremy. Remind me what services you offer.'

'Proof-reading and copy-editing for aspiring novelists. They send me their manuscripts and – '

'Sorry, Jeremy, but I'm just a simple historian. What exactly is copy-editing?'

Johnson embarked on a detailed exposition of what was involved in the process. Harold interrupted the lecture.

'Jeremy, I've seen the essays that your students write and which you've marked – some of the parents have shown me them – and it seems to me that copy-editing is exactly the process you use when marking their work.'

'Yes, of course, it is. It's a precise method of showing them their faulty syntax, grammar and punctuation, and –'

'But regardless of the subject that's being taught, surely every lecturer should engage in constructive criticism of a student's work? Praise what's good about it, make positive suggestions about how it could be improved? Maybe take each student aside, listen to what they have to say, and discuss the essay with them?'

'That would be too time-consuming. I need to – '

'I'm sorry, Jeremy, but what you've told me simply confirms what I've been told characterises your whole approach to teaching. The main complaint that parents have made is that you fail to engage with the students. Your lectures are just that – lectures. You don't discuss things with them, nor ask for their opinions. If any of them try to ask a question, you shut them up. These are teenage students, for God's sake, not postgraduates, though even if they were, your approach would still be inappropriate.'

Johnson's hands fell from his lapels. Harold was anticipating a vigorous riposte, but he remained silent, and he looked down at his knees.

'It's time I was frank with you, Jeremy. You must be aware that we're having difficulty in continuing to offer arts and humanities subjects. We just can't afford the sort of drop-out rates that occur in your classes. So, I'm giving you till the end of this term to improve your performance. I'll be sitting in on some of your lectures, and Marion Deer will be assessing the way you mark your students' work. If there is no improvement by the end of term, I'll have no alternative but to let you go.'

There was no response from Johnson. He continued to look down at his knees, then began shifting about in his chair, clutching his lap. Then he rose, hesitantly, and shuffled towards the door.

Once there, he turned, and said in a voice that quavered slightly, 'There's no need for all that. I'm resigning. Now.'

He left, closing the door quietly behind him. Harold rose from his chair, and as he did, he glanced down at the one just vacated by Johnson. The seat was wet. *My God, the bugger's pissed himself.*

Fortunately, Harold had his own toilet facility across the corridor, so he went into it, unravelled reels of toilet paper, divided them into two bundles, moistened one bundle under a tap, then returned to his office to undertake the required swabbing and drying operation on the chair seat.

As he bent to his task, he had to smile at what the reaction of his staff would be if they were to see their faculty head engaged in such an activity. The job complete, and the toilet paper consigned to his waste-paper bin, he returned to the toilet to wash his hands, still thinking about Jeremy Johnson.

What an enigma the fellow was. Arrogant and dismissive when he had a captive audience, but verging on shy and uncertain in informal situations. Harold knew nothing about his life outside college, apart from what he'd told him today about his copy-editing venture. He didn't even know if he was married. He'd never mentioned a wife, and nobody in the college had ever seen him in town accompanied by a woman. His appearance pointed to his being single; a wife or partner would never let him go to work dressed so shabbily. Harold's wife certainly wouldn't.

Was the man unwell, perhaps? Maybe his incontinence was the result of a bladder infection, or perhaps something worse? And might his shabby clothes be the result of being hard up? But he claimed to be earning a living from copy-editing.

Harold returned to his office, turned on his computer and logged into LinkedIn. The search for a Jeremy Johnson revealed nobody of that name. He then searched under 'copy editing'. There were numerous individuals and companies listed, but none bore Johnson's name.

What the hell. The fellow had probably invented the whole thing. Harold dismissed him from his thoughts and turned his attention to the forthcoming OFSTED inspection.

Chapter 5

It was break-time. Helen, left in the classroom recently vacated by year four, groaned. Desks and chairs were in disarray, paper was scattered all over them and on the floor, the whiteboard still bore the scrawls executed by Miss Barnard, and the room still reeked of her scent.

She set about putting the room in order before the children returned for their next class. It was to be taught by Rosemary Massey, a lady in late middle age who stood no nonsense from the children and who involved Helen in their education. Sometimes she left Helen in charge of the class while she went to attend to administrative matters.

'I know you'll keep them busy,' she often said, 'and I can trust you to stop them misbehaving.'

Helen liked and respected Mrs Massey. She was one of the old school, a rapidly dying breed. Helen despaired of some of the younger teachers, flush with their newly acquired qualifications, who seemed to think her role was simply to act as a fetcher-and-carrier. Kathy Barnard was typical of these: amongst other things, she taught art and craft, and obviously considered Helen, not being a higher-level assistant, to be incapable of helping her with that. As well as being over-perfumed, she was always heavily made-up, and Helen was tempted to tell her that if she were to pay similar attention to the application of paint on her pupils' papers, then they might start to learn something.

The bell to signal the end of break-time hadn't rung, but Rosemary entered the room.

'Ah, Helen, I thought I'd find you in here. You really ought to take a break, you know.'

'I couldn't leave and let you find all this mess, Rosemary.'

Rosemary subsided gradually into her chair. She was overweight, or 'comfortable' as she called it. Helen thought a more apt description would be comforting. She had certainly comforted her on many occasions, particularly when Jane had been a pupil at the school and was giving problems.

'Well, you're going to have a break now because Mrs Paton was in the staffroom looking for you. She said she'd like a word with you in her office if I can spare you.'

Helen was immediately apprehensive. Mrs Paton was the newly appointed headmistress – no, headteacher they had to be called these days – and Helen had yet to get her measure. She seemed pleasant enough, but it didn't do to get on the wrong side of her, as one teacher, a man nearing retirement, had discovered when he called her 'dear' in a staff meeting.

'Oh no! I wonder what I've done wrong?'

'You've done nothing wrong, Helen, quite the contrary. I think you'll be pleasantly surprised when you hear what she has to say. Go on, off with you! Don't keep her waiting.'

Mrs Paton's office was next to the staffroom. As Helen walked along the corridor towards it, she was still slightly apprehensive but was cheered by the light airiness of the building, which was in marked contrast to the gloomy Victorian edifice which had housed the school when she'd started working there.

Mrs Paton's door was ajar, and she obviously sensed when Helen reached it.

'Is that you, Helen? Come in, please. Take a seat.'

There were two easy chairs in the office, and Mrs Paton moved from behind her desk to take the seat beside Helen, but then rose suddenly.

'Oh, you weren't in the staffroom at break, were you. Does that mean you didn't have a coffee? Would you like a cup?'

Helen said that she'd love one. She watched her boss as she busied herself with the kettle and was struck, not for the first time, by how attractive she was. How old was she? In her early 40s, perhaps? Her dark hair was cropped short, but that served to emphasise her delicate features. Her make-up was discreetly applied. She was dressed in a smart suit with a knee-length skirt: this, with her high heels, showed her shapely legs to advantage. Her figure was that of a woman in her twenties; small waist, firm breasts. She appeared to Helen to be nothing like how most people would imagine a headteacher might look. Helen found it hard not to resent women who were blessed with her advantages.

'Thanks for coming, Helen,' she said as she handed her the coffee. 'Let me reassure you, you have nothing to worry about.' She sat down. 'I'd just like a chat, and I might have some good news for you.'

Good news? That wasn't something Helen was accustomed to. She didn't know what to say.

'How long have you been working here as a classroom assistant, Helen?'

'On and off since 1997.'

'I assume you enjoy it?'

That was a question Helen found hard to answer. Sometimes she did, but recently she'd begun to feel undervalued.

She compromised by saying, 'Most of the time.'

'Helen, I've been talking to Rosemary Massey, and she's full of praise for you. I know you've been colleagues for a long time, and she told me what a difficult time you had when you first started when your daughter was a pupil here.'

'She told you about all that, did she?' Helen was hurt that Rosemary had discussed that matter with the headteacher. She hadn't told her she was going to.

'Look, Helen, would you like to tell me about it? Why did you choose to become a classroom assistant at the same school that your daughter was attending? I'd like to hear it from the horse's mouth.'

Helen was more than discomforted; she found herself in a situation that she always tried to avoid, that of having even to think about Jane. Mrs Paton was gazing at her, but her expression indicated sympathy. Helen had no alternative but to answer. She took a gulp from her coffee cup.

'Take your time, Helen.'

'My daughter was a very difficult child. She was disobedient as a toddler. I was dreading the day she'd have to start school. I knew she'd misbehave and get into trouble. So, when the chance of a classroom assistant's post at the school came up, I grabbed it. If Jane knew I was on the premises, she'd be more likely to behave.'

'But you were only here part-time. What did you think might happen when you weren't here?'

'I told her that Rosemary Massey would let me know if she misbehaved, and that if she did, she'd be for it. I told Rosemary that as well.'

'And did that work?'

'Most of the time.'

'Did you actually assist in the classes which Jane attended?'

'No. But I got to hear about the occasions when she played up.'

'And what did you do about that?'

'I gave her a good telling off, of course. And sometimes sent her to bed without any supper.'

Where was all this leading, Helen wondered? Why was she being asked all this? What business was it of Mrs Paton's? It *had* been necessary to use strict discipline with Jane; it was the only way she could be made to behave. The punishments continued when she became a teenager. *I did the right thing, didn't I?* But she was finding this conversation distressing. To her horror, she felt a tear running down her cheek.

Mrs Paton leaned over and touched her hand. 'I'm so sorry to have upset you, Helen. I just needed you to confirm things that I'd heard. Are you okay to carry on?'

Helen nodded, though she was dreading what might be coming next.

'You've got a degree in English Literature, haven't you, Helen? Had you never thought about getting a qualification in education so you could become a teacher rather than just an assistant?'

'I had to bring up a child, didn't I? My husband wasn't much help with that. By the time Jane left secondary school, I was 43, too old to think about returning to college. And anyway, my husband didn't earn enough for me to be able give up this job. He still doesn't.'

'I'll come straight to the point, Helen. You are an experienced and accomplished teaching assistant. You have much that the newly qualified teachers here can learn from you. With a degree, you don't need to attend a college to gain qualified teacher status. This can be achieved by assessing you here in the school. You could then become a full-time teacher and get a salary, payable in the holidays, of course. What do you think about that?'

Helen's mind was a complete blank. It was as though she'd suddenly been told she'd won the lottery but couldn't bring herself to believe it.

'Sorry, this has obviously come as a shock to you. Would you some time to think about it? And no doubt you'll want to discuss it with your husband?'

'Yes, I'd like a few days, please.'

'I hope you'll say yes, Helen. You'll be an invaluable member of staff.'

Mrs Paton got up. The interview was obviously over.

As she walked back down the corridor, Helen's mind was no longer a blank. As soon as Mrs Paton had suggested she might need to discuss the matter with her husband, her thoughts had turned to how she'd enjoy telling Jeremy her news.

*

It was still raining, as it seemed to have been doing all March, but Jeremy, hurrying back home from the college, didn't notice it. If asked to describe his feelings, he would have been unable to give a coherent response. Anger certainly, humiliation to an extent, but also regret that he hadn't told Harold Fletcher exactly what he felt about him and his staff. And there was also a sense of relief that he'd no longer be exposed to all the mediocrity in that so-called educational establishment. At least he'd now be able to give his undivided attention to copy-editing and further develop his business. Yes, he'd get on with that work as soon as he got home.

It was only after he'd slammed shut his front door that he became aware that he was drenched. Cursing, he rubbed his hair with the kitchen towel, then went up to his bedroom, stripped off his clothes and put on a sweater and jogger-bottoms.

At last, he entered his study and waited for the sensation of calm that usually came over him when seated at his computer. But it didn't. Something continued to niggle at him. It suddenly hit him: was he going to tell Helen?

Did he need to tell her? After all, she'd never shown any interest in his job at the college. But how could he explain the fact that he'd no longer be absent from the house for three days each week? He supposed he could ostensibly leave for the college but instead go to the library to do his copy-editing. But he wouldn't have access to his computer there, would he? He couldn't cope with the hi-tech machines in the library, and, in any case, their screens were too small. Even on his own computer, he was finding things increasingly hard to read. His varifocal spectacles were useless when trying to focus on something about two feet away.

He'd just logged on when he heard the front door being slammed. What was Helen doing, getting home so early?

'I'm home!' was shouted up the stairs.

'Okay!' he shouted back.

'Can you come down here? I've got something to tell you.'

Jeremy was instantly apprehensive. Usually, they had little of importance to tell each other because nothing out of the ordinary ever happened to them, not since Jane had left.

He went downstairs. Helen was in the kitchen. 'I'm making a cup of tea. Do you want one?'

It was rare for her to make such an offer. Jeremy looked at her. Her face was slightly flushed.

He sat down at the table. 'Yes, please. What is it you have to tell me?'

'I was called in to see Mrs Paton this morning.'

'Yes? What was that about?'

Without ceasing to stop her tea-making and not sitting down when that was done, nor once looking at him, she proceeded to tell him. She spoke rapidly and didn't stop to let him ask questions.

'Well, are you going to go ahead with it, then?' he asked when she finally fell silent.

'Yes, I am. I think I'll make quite a good teacher, and when I'm full-time, I'll be paid all through the holidays. I'd like to spend a bit of money on myself for once.' As she said this, her eyes were darting round the kitchen.

The financial implications of what she'd told him were immediately apparent to Jeremy: his own loss of income now mattered much less. He came to a decision.

'Well, *I've* got some news for *you*.'

'What's that, then?'

'I've resigned from my job at the college.'

'You've *what*?'

'Well, I've decided I want to concentrate on – '

'What about the money?' This was shouted, and she was staring at him fixedly, something she rarely did. 'How d'you think we're going to manage without it?'

'But if you're going to work full-time and get paid during the holidays, we'll be able to manage, won't we? We won't need my income, and – '

'You *bastard*! You didn't know about me being able to get a full-time job, but you still went ahead and resigned, didn't you?' She was now standing at the sink and screaming. 'Would you have told me if I hadn't told you my news first? I bet you wouldn't! Well, if you're not going to be working, you're going to have to do all the housework and the shopping 'cos I won't have time. I'll be the sole breadwinner, won't I?'

Jeremy rose from his chair.

'Helen, please calm down and listen. I will still be working because I'll be concentrating fully on writing my novel. Of course, I'll be able to help with the housework sometimes, but I'm at a crucial stage with this novel and – '

'Your novel? Your bloody novel! That's all you think about! I've just been offered something life-changing for me, and you haven't shown the slightest interest! Just like you never showed any interest in helping me cope with your daughter. You … you…'

She slumped into a chair, put her elbows on the table, and then, with her head in her hands, began wailing. Jeremy could never cope with that. He left the kitchen and hurried upstairs to his study.

As he sat in front of his computer, he could still hear Helen crying, and the fact she was doing so in the kitchen with its shabby furniture, outdated and dirty equipment, cobweb-festooned ceiling and grease-smeared un-swept floor brought home to him the disaster that was his domestic situation.

Concentrate on something else, he told himself. His computer was still turned on, so he logged on to Colonel Collinson's autobiography. He scan-read his latest offering and began to consider ways in which the turgid prose might be enlivened. Occasionally, his thoughts returned to the scene in the kitchen, and he became aware that Helen was no longer crying. She'd probably soon go to bed, as she often did when upset. He'd stay up here for a while, then return to the kitchen to heat up a ready meal for himself.

He gradually became immersed in the Colonel's manuscript, but suddenly he sensed the door behind him being opened. He half rose from his chair but got no further because he was knocked sideways by a blow to his ear. He tried to right himself, but his other ear was struck. The pain was intense, all-consuming, and he hardly registered his hair being grasped until he was pulled by it from the chair and knocked to the floor. He was kicked, first in the stomach, then in the genitals. Such was his agony that he could only gasp. He could do nothing but lay there and hope that the assault would soon be over.

Chapter 6

Helen was walking to school, battling against the gusty wind and rain. Why weren't winters like they used to be, she wondered, with days of frosty calm sunshine? Everyone had been complaining for months about the perpetual gloom of this depressing season, as indeed had she.

But she was more cheerful today. Foremost in her mind was the anticipation of telling Mrs Paton that she had decided to take up her offer. She was eager to witness the pleasure on Mrs Paton's face and to learn more about the nature of the assessment and how long it would take before she was fully qualified and able to start working full-time. At last, she would have a satisfying job in line with her abilities, something in which she could immerse herself and help her forget the catastrophe that was her marriage.

Mrs Paton had agreed to see her just after the morning break, so Helen decided to visit the staffroom beforehand to have a celebratory coffee. It wasn't crowded when she entered, and chairs next to Rosemary Massey were vacant. She went across and sat down.

'Rosemary, I didn't get a chance to thank you for the good word you put in for me with Mrs Paton.'

'That's all right, my dear. Have you decided to take up her offer?'

'Yes, I have. I'm going to see her after break.'

While they were speaking, Kathy Barnard walked over and sat down opposite them. Helen noticed her skirt was even shorter than usual, and she crossed her legs slowly and expansively, no doubt, thought Helen, hoping to get the attention of the two young male members of staff standing nearby.

'Oh, Kathy, isn't it wonderful?' said Rosemary, 'Helen's going for qualified teacher status. She'll probably soon be working here full-time.'

Kathy Barnard sniffed. 'So, who's going to help me clear up the classroom after I've finished my lessons?'

'Help you?' said Helen, 'I wasn't aware I ever do that. It's a job you always leave me to do by myself.'

Kathy Barnard immediately rose, walked over to her two male colleagues, and began talking to them.

'Well said, Helen!' said Rosemary. 'That young woman needs taking down a peg or two.'

Helen was amazed that she'd spoken to that Barnard woman the way she had. Was she already acting in the way that she might when she became a qualified teacher? There were quite a few of the younger teachers who, in Rosemary's words, needed to be taken down a peg or two. And she'd find this easier to do when she had the money to dress more smartly and have a proper hairdo – perhaps even have it dyed so she was blonde again? Maybe that would stop them demeaning her.

She was feeling less positive when she left Mrs Paton's office. The headteacher had expressed delight that she'd decided to go ahead, but when she outlined the procedures to be followed, it seemed that the process of assessment might take several months, and it was possible that she might not be able to take up a full-time post until the start of the next academic year. But it would be possible to increase her hours if that was acceptable.

Better than nothing, Helen supposed, but it would mean more months of confinement with an unemployed Jeremy. Whatever regrets she had about slapping and kicking him the previous evening evaporated. He deserved it. She was in no mood to return to the staffroom and set off home. At least the rain had eased a bit.

As she neared home, resentment towards Jeremy swelled. She would never forgive him for how in their final year at university he'd taken advantage of her, when for the first time in her life, her moral code had temporarily deserted her. And if he'd loved her, which he'd claimed he did, why had he voiced so many misgivings about getting married when she'd revealed she was pregnant? And why, when Jane had been born, had he distanced himself from her upbringing? And why… The questions she was asking herself were endless, and she was still posing them as she reached her front door.

*

Jeremy had waited until Helen had left the house before he made any attempt to get up. He'd hardly slept at all. His stomach and testicles were still aching from her assault. He should have seen it coming, even though her outbursts of rage had diminished since Jane had left.

The kitchen was even more filthy than usual; no doubt she had deliberately engineered this before leaving. He made himself a cup of tea – his aching stomach made him retch at the thought of food – and carried it up to his study. The place still seemed tainted by her presence the previous evening.

He eased himself onto his chair and turned on the computer. He still had the offerings from Stephanie Bridges and Colonel Collinson to read and copy-edit. Usually, he would start with Stephanie's, but today the idea of reading anything written by a woman did not appeal, so he opened Collinson's attachment.

It seemed to be as usual – an almost day-by-day account of his time serving in the army, all written with clumsy syntax and totally devoid of scene-setting or the use of imagery. It could only be described as a diary.

He required not just a copy-editor, but a ghost-writer. Could this be another service he could offer? He might then receive a share of the royalties in the unlikely event of Collinson's book being published.

But as he continued reading, he began to be intrigued. Collinson was giving an account of his time serving in Northern Ireland at the time of the Troubles. There was a long anti-IRA diatribe after he'd heard about the

Birmingham pub bombings, and then – Jeremy was amazed by what he'd written next:

Told Sgt Jones we must take revenge. We knew about a local Provisional called Murphy O'Connor, so I said we ought to kill the bastard. We followed him the next day in the Land Rover. When he got to an empty street, we bundled him in and drove off into the countryside. Jones thumped him in the head to keep him quiet. When we got to a wood, we pulled him out and beat him up. Then, I shot him in the balls. Then in the head. We dumped his body in some bushes and drove off. Serve the bastard right. We ought to do that to all the Provos we know about.

Was Collinson deliberately out to shock? Was it really his intention to have this autobiography published? Surely, he must know that after the Good Friday Agreement, there'd been investigations into those in the British army who'd taken the law into their own hands?

Jeremy needed time away to consider what he should do next. He got up and went downstairs, no longer aware of the mess in the kitchen around which he paced, debating the options open to him. He could, of course, simply continue the editing. After all, it was not within his remit to advise a client about the legal implications of what had been written.

He came to a decision. He needed to contact Collison to tell him about the reservations he had before he could continue with editing. He charged up to the study, as he did so becoming aware that he was still in his pyjamas and dressing gown and hadn't washed or shaved this morning.

He logged on and was about to compose his email to Collinson but heard the front door slam. What the hell was she doing back this early? Wasn't she intending to be at the school all morning? He was damned if he was going down to greet her.

He didn't need to. He heard her running up the stairs. His door flew open.

'Trying to make a point, are you? Leaving all that mess downstairs? And you haven't even got dressed! You idle slob! Is this what I'm going to have to put up with when I start working full-time? Feeling sorry for yourself, are you? You deserve everything you got!'

She turned and marched out.

He was in no mood to email Collinson now. He sank back in his chair, feeling listless and at the same time restless. For the first time, it occurred to him that now he was unemployed, he was totally devoid of face-to-face contact with anyone, apart from Helen, of course, something he wanted to avoid. Okay, he hadn't cared for the company of the other staff at the F.E. college, but he was now without the stimulation he felt when delivering lectures to students. And he certainly wouldn't be welcome back at the Rebel Writers' group. For the first time in years, he considered visiting the local pub, the *Bricklayers Arms*. Anything to get out of the house.

There was no point in arguing with Helen. He decided, yes, he *would* visit the *Bricklayers*. He'd go there as soon as he'd had dinner and washed, shaved, and dressed. He might even have a few shorts to help him build up some Dutch courage for when he returned later.

Chapter 7

In the days when Jeremy had occasionally visited the *Bricklayers Arms* many years ago, it still bore the semblance of being the respectable working-man's pub that it probably always had been, with a public bar occupied mainly by old men and a saloon bar frequented by younger men with their lady friends. He used to drink his shandy in the public bar, ignored by the old fellows whose conversation seemed to be limited to football and what had been on the box the previous night. He was apprehensive about going there now, because he didn't know what sort of establishment it had become. Suppose it was now a haunt for youngsters, all standing and shouting to be heard over blaring music, the two genders ogling each other? Or maybe it had gone up-market with plush seating and a clientele to match? He'd feel uncomfortable in such a setting because of his shabby clothes. He'd never before worried about how he looked; he had more elevated things to occupy his mind, but now he was only too aware of his reduced financial circumstances.

His evening meal with Helen had been eaten in total silence.

But when he'd put on his overcoat, Helen had shouted, 'Going out, are you? Well, I don't care where you're going, but you'd better do the washing up when you get home because I'm damned if I'm going to do it.' He hadn't replied and slammed the front door behind him.

For once, it wasn't raining outside, but there was still a bitter wind which penetrated his threadbare overcoat. One good thing about the appalling weather, it kept the yobs off the streets. When he reached the pub, he was relieved to see that its exterior had changed very little apart from a new sign above the entrance. He entered the lobby, and yes, the door to his right was still labelled 'Public Bar'. He pushed it open and was confronted by a vast television screen and assailed by a blaring commentary on what was probably a football match. He had a vague impression of trestle tables, stools and settles occupied mainly by men, not talking but gawping at the TV. It was no longer the place in which to have a quiet drink. He backed out and turned towards the other door.

This was labelled 'Lounge' rather than, as he had been expecting, 'Saloon Bar'. He was apprehensive about what he might find. Might there be plush armchairs beside low tables, maybe each with its own lamp, a deep-pile carpet, waiter service perhaps? Hesitantly, he opened the door.

He needn't have worried. The room was brightly lit from above, hard-backed chairs were grouped round the tables, and the clientele seemed to comprise middle-aged people in couples or groups of four. There weren't many of them. He walked to the bar, asked for a shandy and a small Scotch, and was served by a smiling woman of indeterminate age who addressed him as 'sir'.

He sat down at a table at the side of the lounge and began to relax. He started watching and listening to the other occupants of the room. There was no background music, so he could hear those sitting nearest to him quite clearly. Their speech had the not-quite-cockney accents typical of the Watford working-classes of their generation, an accent which, amongst youngsters, had been superseded by Estuary English, itself now influenced by the speech patterns of third-generation Caribbeans. Some of Jeremy's students had spoken like that, and one of them had dared to address him as 'Bro'.

Jeremy was fascinated by accents and speech patterns. In his novels, he prided himself on his sensitive portrayal of his characters and gave each a distinct way of speaking. He became so engrossed in listening to the locals and thinking about accents that he was surprised to find he'd finished both his drinks. He must have enjoyed them, so he decided to have another shandy.

The room had filled up somewhat, and he had to wait at the bar to be served. While standing there, he could overhear the conversation between two couples sitting at the table behind him. They were speaking the Queen's English! It seemed the pub was not the sole preserve of the hoi-polloi after all. He sneaked a glance at them – they were elderly, casually dressed, but the women had obviously taken pains with their hair and make-up.

He carried his drinks back to his table. He had a clear view of the two couples sitting near the bar, but they were too distant for their conversation to be heard. Pity: he would have liked to know what they might be discussing, given that they seemed somewhat misplaced in this environment. Their conversation was frequently interrupted by audible guffaws.

As he watched them, he became aware that there was something familiar about one of the men, the way his shoulders moved when he laughed. He was sitting with his back to Jeremy, so Jeremy had only glimpses of his profile when he turned to talk to one of the women. But then he got up, collected glasses from the table and walked with them to the bar. He was very tall and had a slight stoop – My God, could it be …? When he reached the bar, he had to wait for service and turned to face the room – yes! Jim Ellison!

Jim had been Jeremy's colleague when he first joined the college; in fact, he'd been Jeremy's immediate senior, being the only other English lecturer and of many years standing. They'd had little in common. Jim had been in his late 40s then, so he must be approaching 70 now. But he'd aged well; he had a full head of hair, albeit almost white.

Jim had to make two trips to carry the drinks from the bar to his table. On the second trip, he happened to look across the room. His glance fell on Jeremy, and there was obviously immediate recognition because he almost dropped the glasses. He placed them on the table, spoke briefly to one of the women, and walked across the room towards Jeremy.

'Jeremy Johnson! It is you, isn't it?'

Jeremy stood up. They shook hands.

'I've never seen you in here before. D'you come here a lot?'

'Haven't been in here for years. It's the nearest pub to my house, and tonight I fancied a drink. What about you?'

'Oh, Fred and Alice, the couple we're with, live quite close by. How are you keeping, Jeremy?'

'I'm well, thank you. And you?'

'Mustn't grumble, as my old mum used to say. Look, it would be nice to catch up. Mind if I bring my drink over and sit with you for a bit?'

'Won't your wife mind?'

'Jenny? Of course not. With you in a minute.'

As Jim walked over to get his drink, Jeremy was thinking he should have said he had to get home; he didn't relish talking about old times at the college with Jim. Jim had never approached his subject with the seriousness that it deserved, and he'd been far too pally with the students.

'So, Jeremy, do you see any of the old crowd from the college?' Jim asked as he sat down opposite him.

'No, the people we knew all must have left years ago.'

'Anyway, Jeremy, what have you been doing with yourself for the past twenty years? None of us ever knew if you'd left to get another lecturing job.'

'Oh, I'm self-employed. A novelist.'

Was that a flicker of a grin the passed over Jim's features? If it was, he disguised it by taking a hearty quaff of beer.

'Are you, by God? What sort of novels do you write – no, let me guess. Fantasy? Sci-Fi? Thrillers?'

'Certainly not! Nothing like that at all.'

'Well, maybe detective stories? Or romance? Or erotic novels, perhaps? Those sell well, so I've been told. Made your fortune from them, have you?'

This was said with a perfectly straight face. Jeremy was unsure whether he was being mocked, as he sometimes had been when Jim had spoken to him at work. But he decided to take his questions at face value.

'No, I write literary fiction. My books are based on characterisation and character development. So, none of my characters are given clear goals in the stories. They're full of ambiguities. I write about their inner journeys and their psychological setbacks. The endings of my novels are inconclusive because I try to make them reflect the uncertainties that most people experience in their journeys through life. I trust that my readers are seeking not escapism but are more interested in ideas.'

'Got a lot of readers, have you? What are your books' titles? I've never come across anything written by you.'

'That's because I write under a nom-de-plume.'

'Which is?'

'Enough about me, Jim. What have you been doing since you retired?'

'Oh, I keep busy. See a lot of the grandchildren, bless 'em. Try to keep fit – I walk about four miles a day. Recently, I've been listening to a lot of my old CDs: those rock and blues bands of the 60s and 70s were really innovative. And some of the lyrics written by the likes of Lennon, McCartney and Ray Davies are pure poetry.'

'Poetry? Are you serious?'

'Yes! I used to get our students to read them. Of course, the Beatles and the Kinks were ancient history to them, but their lyrics reach across the generations. Some of their sentiments were amazingly mature for fellows who were only in their twenties.'

'I can't say I've ever heard them. I never listen to popular music, never did.'

Jim took a swig of his beer and looked at Jeremy appraisingly. 'Well, Jeremy, maybe if you had, you might have found it easier to relate to your students.'

'But I doubt that would have gained me their respect. They were there to learn things outside their limited experiences which would help them pass their examinations.'

Jim stared unsmilingly at Jeremy on hearing this and shifted in his seat as though about to get up and leave, but eventually, he spoke. 'Anyway, Jeremy, what else do you do with your time when you're not writing novels?'

Jeremy began telling him about his proof-reading and copy-editing business. He didn't need to explain to Jim what copy-editing entailed. Jim seemed interested and asked about the sort of novels that his clients submitted. Jeremy was disparaging about Stephanie Bridges' efforts, and Jim nodded in apparent sympathy. But when he began telling him about the recent submission from Colonel Collinson and his concerns about it, Jim interrupted.

'How are going to respond to him, then?'

'Oh, I'll send him an email telling him about my reservations, but –'

'Email? Why don't you phone him? He sounds an interesting character.'

'I don't have his phone number.'

'Well, why don't you ask him for it? No, better than that, why don't you arrange to meet him?'

'I don't think it's advisable to meet up with clients. One has to remain dispassionate, and – '

'But if the fellow's writing his autobiography, don't you think it would be an advantage to find out what makes him tick? That might make it easier for you to advise him.'

Jeremy made to take a sip of shandy but discovered his glass was empty. He was finding the conversation with Jim enlivening and hadn't been conscious of drinking. It was heartening to talk to someone who seemed to find his work interesting. Perhaps he'd misjudged Jim?

'Well?' said Jim, 'Are you going to think about it? Meeting him, I mean.'

Jeremy realised he didn't need to think about it: the prospect of face-to-face contact with someone other than Helen was suddenly very inviting.

'Yes, I will try to meet him, Jim. Thanks for suggesting it. If he agrees, I'll let you know what transpired, if you'd like to meet up again.'

'Yes, why not?'

'Can I get you a drink, Jim?'

'Thanks for the offer, but I'd better get back to the missus.'

He stood up and offered Jeremy his hand. Jeremy found himself grasping it as though it were a lifeline. After Jim had walked back to his wife, Jeremy sat for a while, relishing the evening he'd had. It was only when he got up to leave that he became conscious that his bladder was full. He just managed to make it to the gents in time. As he stood at the urinal, in his head he was composing the email he'd send to Collinson. He could hardly wait to get home to his computer, and it was only when he reached his front door that he remembered that home contained Helen.

PART TWO - SPRING

Chapter 8

Jeremy was on a Chiltern Line train bound for Aylesbury.

Partly because of his poor eyesight, he was blind to the passing landscape, but in any case, he was only ever concerned with his immediate surroundings. On the few occasions that he travelled, he rarely looked up from whatever he was reading other than to check the name of the stations at which the train stopped. Today he was immersed in the Times Literary Supplement, though the juddering of the train meant that he had constantly to adjust his posture so the lower parts of his varifocal spectacles were aligned with the paper.

But he *was* aware of the weather. The constant cloud and rain of February and March through which he'd had to walk first to the F.E. college, then to the library, had recently given way to warm sunshine. For most people, this was the harbinger of spring with all the seasonal delights that it afforded, but for Jeremy, this simply meant that he could dispense with his shabby overcoat.

The train slowed. Jeremy glanced up – ah, yes, Amersham. He still had some way to go, but perhaps he ought to be giving more thought to his forthcoming meeting, even though he'd rehearsed how he might approach it many times over the past fortnight.

He wasn't conscious of people boarding the train until a portly man sat down opposite him – why? There were plenty of vacant seats along the carriage.

'Hope you don't mind me sitting here,' the man said, 'but I like to be by the window.' He made himself comfortable, which involved him spreading his legs to such an extent that Jeremy was forced to shift to the seat adjacent to the gangway. The train pulled out, and Jeremy returned to reading the TLS.

'Only a few more weeks, and then the bluebells will appear,' said the man.

'Eh?' Jeremy raised his eyes. The man was peering through the window.

'Bluebells. They come out a lot earlier than they used to. Global warming, of course. Then the beech leaves will follow. There's nothing to beat the Chilterns in spring. It's the combination of the chalk bedrock and the clay that covers it that makes it so unique.'

'Really?'

'Yes. Look at that beautiful valley. Are you from round these parts?'

'No.'

'Well, see that mansion over there? It's called Shardeloes. It used to be the home of the squires of Amersham. We have a former squire to thank that the railway didn't cut through the valley back in the 1890s. It would have been followed by housing for commuters. He was an MP and managed to get the route changed so it avoided the old town and the valley because he didn't want it to spoil his view.'

'Is that so?' Jeremy folded up his TLS and resigned himself to being bored for the remainder of his journey.

'Yes. Pity a squire doesn't live there now because that damned HS2 is going to cut right through the valley. They've already started working on it.'

Jeremy didn't have an opinion about high-speed rail, so he was unable to comment. The fellow was probably one of those environmentalists. Jeremy prepared to be subjected to a lecture. He didn't like being lectured to by the self-important. He felt like telling the man that he ought to do some walking through the valley in order to lose some weight.

'Of course,' the fellow continued, 'this line descends into the valley to carry on up to Wendover. Fortunately, it by-passes Little Missenden, which remains unscathed. It's a charming village and ...'

Jeremy was instantly alert. Little Missenden! That was where his father had been born and spent his childhood. When Jeremy was a child in Luton, his father had droned on interminably about Little Missenden and the countryside around it. But then his father had droned on about many things, few of them of interest to Jeremy. He began thinking about his father and became deaf to the remarks of his travelling companion until he rose from his seat.

'Wendover!' he announced. 'My stop. You're bound for Aylesbury, I assume?'

'Yes.'

'Well, I don't envy you. The place has gone downhill rapidly in recent years. I'll bid you goodbye.'

Jeremy chose not to return to his window seat. His was the next stop but one. He was amused by the description that the departing man had given to Aylesbury; they were precisely the same words which Helen had used when he'd told her where he was bound; she'd been quoting her mother, recently dead, who'd lived in nearby Bicester.

Jeremy and Helen had come to some sort of accommodation. They were now reasonably polite with each other. Jeremy found it easier sharing a house with her now her teaching hours had been increased and she spent less time there. He'd told her about his copy-editing venture and that he was going to visit Collinson.

'Well, it had better bring in some money,' had been her response, and he'd taken great satisfaction in telling her that Collinson had also agreed to pay his train fare.

The train began to slow down. He picked up his briefcase and prepared to get off. His thoughts turned to how he should approach his meeting with Colonel Collinson. He was looking forward to it.

He was having to walk from the station to Collinson's house. It had taken numerous email exchanges before Collinson had finally agreed to meet him. He'd given

Jeremy his address and said that he lived a ten-minute taxi ride from the station but had refused to pay the taxi fare – 'I'm not made of money, Mr Rennie', he'd written. Jeremy was therefore obliged to walk and had to purchase a street map at the station. He doubted that Collinson would agree to pay for that.

Jeremy's map-reading skills were poor. He'd hated geography when he was at school; it was purely factual and descriptive, a subject which, in his opinion, appealed only to those pupils devoid of imagination. It took him a long time to work out that he had to make his way to the town centre before navigating his way along the streets that led to Collinson's house. Crossing the town centre was in itself a problem because it was pedestrianised and without direction signs.

At last, he reached a road which was named on his map. He had difficulty in equating inches on a map to distance on the ground but thought Collinson's house was probably about fifteen minutes' walk away. He was glad he'd invested in a pack of incontinence pads in preparation for his journey, though they weren't items for which he could charge Collinson.

He had a mental image of the man Collinson was likely to be. An ex-colonel, so probably quite well-off; formally dressed, florid complexion resulting from whisky consumption, a moustache, and no doubt an abrupt manner - his autobiography and his emails certainly pointed to that. But Jeremy had no worries about being awed. It was he who had the literary expertise, and once he'd impressed the colonel with that, he could raise the matter of the risks inherent in publishing his memoir.

When he reached Collinson's street, he was surprised to find the houses along it were modest semi-detached, having assumed that a former colonel would have a grander home. He pressed the button of the doorbell. After a wait of several minutes, the door opened, and he was confronted by a thin man with a pronounced stoop leaning on a walking stick. He was wearing a baggy sweater and shapeless corduroy trousers. Apart from sparse strands of white hair that fell over his ears, he was bald.

'Mr Rennie, I assume? Come in. Come through to the kitchen. I was about to have a cup of tea. Would you care for one?' His voice was quiet and quavered slightly.

In one respect, the kitchen reminded Jeremy of his own: all the equipment in it was outdated. But apart from a few items of crockery in the drainer, the room was tidy and clean. Maybe the fellow had a cleaner?

It took some time for Collinson to make the tea, but eventually the two were seated on uncomfortable Windsor chairs in front of a Formica table. Collinson didn't speak; he seemed to be having difficulty in swallowing his tea. Jeremy decided to open the conversation.

'Colonel – '

'Call me Eustace, please,' was spluttered as tea ran down his chin.

'Very well. Call me Albert. Eustace, thank you for agreeing to see me. There are some things which we need to clarify before I continue copy-editing your work.'

'What are they?'

'Well, the first problem is the style in which it's written. It reads more like a diary written in haste than an autobiography, and – '

'That's because it *is* a diary.'

'You mean you've just copied your original diary verbatim?'

Collinson wiped the tea from his chin and cleared his throat. His rheumy eyes were staring at Jeremy.

'Yes, almost. I wanted to show how I felt at the time I wrote it. I wanted it to read like I spoke and thought, don't y'know. I can't be doing with fancy embellishments.'

Well, that went some way to explaining the abrupt nature of the emails he'd sent. But before pursuing the issue of writing style, Jeremy decided to address the matter that most concerned him.

'Col … Eustace, if your diary is ever published, have you considered the implications for you of some of the things you've written? I'm referring in particular to your time in Northern Ireland at the time of the Troubles. You could find *yourself* in serious trouble.'

'Yes, I'm well aware of that.'

'I don't understand. Why should you want to – '

'I want to get it all off my chest!' His gaze then left Jeremy and sank to the tabletop. 'In any case, I won't find myself in trouble. I've decided I'd like it to be published posthumously. I haven't got long, you see.'

Jeremy was at a loss. He had no idea how to respond to Collinson's revelation of his impending death. He was struggling for a way to turn the discussion to how the autobiography might be improved when Collinson began talking.

'I never wanted to join the army. I went to public school, y'see, and it was expected that those of us who weren't brainy enough to go to university should think about training to be an officer. And my father insisted I join up.'

'So you didn't enjoy the training?'

'Oh, that wasn't so bad. In fact, I even made a few friends. Never had any friends at school, y'know.'

'Why was that, Eustace?'

'Because all the fellows in my dorm could talk about was girls and popular music, yes, even public schoolboys. This was the late 1950's, y'see. But I wasn't interested in all that. My father had kept me on a tight rein.'

Collinson's voice had lost its quaver, and he was becoming almost animated. He was maintaining eye contact with Jeremy, who'd begun to realise that there might be some similarities in their adolescence.

'Tell me more about your time in the army, Eustace.'

'Well, as soon as I finished officer training, I was put in charge of a squad. That's when it all started to go wrong for me. I couldn't get on with the squaddies, y'see. Foul-mouthed working-class types. Told dirty jokes all the time. It was obvious they had no respect for me.'

'Didn't you consider leaving?'

'What other job could I have done? Anyway, to go on, we were sent to Northern Ireland. The Troubles were well under way. The Bogside Catholics made it clear they loathed us, did all sorts of things to get us riled. The squaddies hated them; they started ranting about them and the Provos. I agreed with all they said, so I started joining in, started using their sort of language. I think they began to respect me more.'

'And did you find yourself getting to like them?'

'In a way. A lot of what they said was Double Dutch to me, of course. But they were patriotic chaps, don't y'know. And then the Birmingham pub bombings occurred. We were all outraged. The men said we should grab one of the local Provos and get our revenge. If I'd gone against that, I'd have lost their respect. So that was how I found myself leading what was a murder squad.'

'So you didn't really want to do that?' asked Jeremy.

'I did at the time because it gained me kudos with my troops. But after the Good Friday Agreement, I began to get a conscience. What I did has haunted me ever since. So, I'm writing about it. You know why, don't you?'

Jeremy wasn't sure that he did.

'Atonement!' Eustace shouted. Then he fell silent and remained so and stared down at the tabletop.

'Excuse me, Eustace, could you point me in the direction of your toilet?'

'Top of the stairs. It's the door facing you.'

Not only did Jeremy need to relieve himself, but he needed a few minutes alone to consider what advice to give Eustace – he was surprised to find he was thinking of him by that name and not Collinson. He dropped his trousers and underpants to check his incontinence pad. It was only slightly damp. He urinated, and while he was washing his hands, an idea came to him, something that Eustace might find acceptable.

He returned to the kitchen to find Eustace engaged in the slow process of making more tea. He asked Jeremy if he'd like another cup, and Jeremy was about to refuse when he realised that he could risk it. Wearing an incontinence pad was proving to be a liberating experience.

Eustace placed a cup in front of him. 'Sorry I can't offer you a biscuit or anything,' he said. 'I'm out of stock. My carer won't be here with the shopping until this afternoon.'

'Don't worry about that, Eustace. Look, let me be frank: in its present form, your book's unpublishable. That's because it goes into endless details about mundane day-to-day events, most of which would be of no interest to a reader.'

'Oh dear. So, you can't help me then?

'Yes, I can. I suggest that much of the book is re-written in narrative form, maybe by a third-person narrator, and – '

'But I can't do that! Wouldn't know where to start! I'm not an author, am I?'

'Hang on a bit. What you *can* do is interpose verbatim extracts from your diary when these give accounts of action scenes – like the killing of the Provo – because these would engage the reader.'

'But I'd still have to re-write the rest, and I know I can't do that.'

'There's no need for you to do that, Eustace. I'll do it.'

There was no immediate response. He just stared at Jeremy.

'Are you serious?' he said eventually. 'You're offering to write the book for me?'

'Well, part of it. And it'll be based on your diaries but with a lot cut out and with a bit of embellishment to make the remainder more interesting.'

'So you'd be my … what's the word … co-author?'

'No. I'll be what's called a ghost writer. If it's published, you'll be named as the sole author, though, of course, I'd appreciate an acknowledgement of my help on the title page.'

'But, Albert, how much will you charge for that service?'

'Well, how do you feel about this?'

On the train on his way home, Jeremy was as near to being contented as he had ever been. It had been one of the most enjoyable days he could remember having. He'd agreed to charge Eustace only a little more than his usual copy-editing rates on the understanding that if the book were to be published after Eustace's death, it would be he who would receive the royalties. The old chap obviously had nobody else to leave his money to, apart from his carer perhaps.

But it wasn't just the prospect of potential financial reward that was cheering him. He'd come to like Eustace. Once they'd agreed on the details of how they'd proceed, the old boy had relaxed and began talking about his life. He'd never married, and after leaving the army, he'd not kept up with the few friends he'd made in it. He was now essentially completely alone, apart from his carer, who visited him most days. While Jeremy had been talking with Eustace, he'd felt a growing empathy with him. Despite the disparity of their backgrounds, there was perhaps the beginning of a friendship; after all, they'd now be in frequent contact with a shared objective, for Eustace had invited him to continue visiting him, rather than them just emailing each other.

He began to consider if similar enjoyment might come from personal contact with his other client.

Chapter 9

'Rosemary, I'm sorry this is so late. I know you must be wanting to get home. I had so many other members of staff to see today.'

'That's all right, Mrs Paton, I was in no hurry.'

'Oh, please call me Jennifer. No need for ceremony when you're in here.'

Rosemary, sitting opposite Mrs Paton in her office, was amused. Mrs Paton – she couldn't think of her as Jennifer – was, despite her relative youth, insistent that her staff observed formalities when interacting with each other in front of the children. But this rule was relaxed when one was in her office unless, of course, misdemeanours were being addressed. Not that Rosemary had ever been called in for such a matter, but some of the junior staff-members had, and Mrs Paton had acquired a reputation amongst them for severity. Rosemary had overheard Kathy Barnard refer to her as a bossy bitch.

'I'd like a chat with you about Helen Johnson. It's been two months now since I increased her hours, and she'll soon be getting assessment visits from the university. How d'you think she's getting on?'

Rosemary, as Helen's mentor, had long been aware that she would at some point be asked this question but was no nearer being sure she could give an honest response. She hesitated, uncertain how to start.

'Well, she obviously puts a great deal of effort into her lesson preparation. I've seen the notes she makes. And that's not just for Keystage 2 pupils; she's just as assiduous in preparing for teaching the infants.'

'Yes, I'm sure she's very conscientious. How is she in front of the class?'

'She's very good with the reception classes. She makes it clear who's boss, but she engages with them fully and is sympathetic to the slow learners. Because the class knows they mustn't misbehave, she gets no interruptions when she's talking to individuals.'

'And how is she with the older pupils?'

'Well … to be honest, not quite so successful.'

'Go on.'

'Well, those pupils who knew her when she was just a classroom assistant don't behave as well as they might.'

'Are you saying she has problems keeping order?'

'Occasionally. Sometimes she doesn't stay cool, doesn't keep her voice low.'

'You mean she shouts at them?'

'Sometimes. And, of course, that provokes them to behave more badly.'

'I see. D'you think we have a problem here? I've promised her a full-time post next academic year - on your recommendation, if you remember, Rosemary. If she's unable to keep order, I may have to – *oh damn*!'

Mrs Paton's telephone had started ringing.

'Sorry, Rosemary, I'd better take this.' She picked up the phone. 'Hello? Oh, Fred, I'm in a meeting and – '

Rosemary could hear the cockney cadences of the caretaker coming from the receiver.

'Oh Lord. Okay, Fred, I'm on my way.' She put the phone down. 'Awfully sorry, Rosemary, but Fred's caught a boy vandalising the toilets. I'd better go and sort it out. I won't be too long. Would you mind waiting? We need to continue our discussion.'

'No, that's all right.'

'Help yourself to coffee. Only instant at this time of day, I'm afraid.'

Rosemary was glad to have some time to herself; she needed to consider what she should say next. She was torn between adherence to her own professional code and her sympathy for Helen. She hadn't been entirely frank with Mrs Paton, for Helen didn't just shout at the pupils; occasionally she screamed at them. She'd become a different person from the reserved classroom assistant she'd once been, probably the result of the pressure she was now under. Rumours about her performance in the classroom were whispered in the staffroom, and some of the younger staff members, most noticeably Kathy Barnard, seemed to relish the stress she was under. They'd also started making comments about her appearance. She'd dyed her hair blonde, and it didn't suit her.

Mrs Paton was taking her time. Rosemary decided to take up her offer of a coffee. The jar was probably in the small cabinet on the wall behind her desk. Everything in the cabinet was meticulously arranged, and the jar was easy to find. Milk? Must be in the small fridge on the shelf to the left of the cabinet. Its only contents were a carton of semi-skimmed gluten-free milk and some bottles of water, some of which, Rosemary noticed, were tonic water and – good heavens – behind them was – could it be? Yes, it was! A small bottle of gin! So, the highly professional Mrs Paton had a guilty secret. Did even she sometimes find the pressures of her job such that she needed a boost? Rosemary suddenly felt less in awe of her. While she was making her coffee, she knew she would no longer feel guilty about being economical with the truth. Something had happened yesterday that had shocked her, so much that she had yet to talk to Helen about it. Her affection for Helen had so far prevented her from informing Mrs Paton.

She had been walking along the corridor and heard shouts and screams coming from the classroom where Helen was teaching Year Six. She had entered the room to be confronted with mayhem; very few of the children were seated, most were running round the room whooping. Helen was standing in front of Leila Bridges, and they were screaming at each other. Helen was obviously unaware that Rosemary had entered, for she was advancing on Leila Bridges with her arm raised above her shoulder.

Just in time, Rosemary had shouted, 'Helen!' and silence fell, as did Helen's arm. 'Class dismissed!' Rosemary had said quietly, and the pupils filed out of the room.

'Sorry to have been so long.' Mrs Paton had returned. Rosemary hadn't registered the clicking of her high heels as she walked along the corridor.

'It was that little devil John Pearce. Fred caught him scrawling on toilet wall. I think I'll have to get his parents in – oh, good, I see you've made yourself a coffee. I think I'll have one.'

'The milk's here,' said Rosemary.

'Oh, right.'

Rosemary noticed a flicker of a frown on her brow. Had Mrs Paton just realised that her secret in the fridge had been discovered?

'Right,' said Mrs Paton as she busied herself making coffee. 'About Helen. What's your honest opinion? Is she really suited to being a teacher? If she isn't, there's no point in her going for qualified teacher status.'

'I think it might be a bit soon to make that decision. Might it be better to give her a few more weeks to adapt to her new situation? She's probably under a lot of stress.'

'Well, teaching's a stressful job, as well you know.'

'Yes, but I've been a teacher for years, and I've become accustomed to the way children have changed over that time.'

Mrs Paton sat down with her coffee. 'What exactly do you mean by that?'

'Well, children mature far more quickly than they used to when I started out. Those in Year 6 are now on the verge of adolescence; in fact, some of the girls already are. They sometimes verge on the rebellious. And the way some of them dress!'

Mrs Paton frowned. 'But they're all in school uniform.'

Rosemary wondered if Mrs Paton was being deliberately disingenuous. Yes, they were in school uniform, but some of their skirts were so short that, were it not for the fact they wore black tights, their knickers would be clearly visible. And those who were well-developed sometimes left the top buttons of their blouses undone.

'Anyway,' said Mrs Paton, 'Helen had a daughter who attended here, didn't she? You've told me about that. Does she tell you anything about her family, her husband? Is her domestic life happy? And what's her husband's job?'

'Her husband's some sort of writer, but she hardly ever speaks about him. Nor about her daughter, Jane, come to that. Her domestic life is a complete mystery to me.'

'Do you know what happened to her daughter after she left here?'

'She went to the comprehensive school up the road. That's all I know. Helen never speaks about her.'

'Hmmm. Well, thanks for your help, Rosemary. I assume you've broached the issue with her and put a plan in place to support her. I'll give her a few more weeks before I come to a decision about her future. I'm sorry to have kept you so long.'

'That's quite alright. Good evening, Mrs … Jennifer.'

Rosemary walked back along the corridor, relieved that Mrs Paton had not pressed her further. She'd spoken the truth, hadn't she? She didn't know anything about Helen's home life. But she did know a little more about daughter Jane – meek and obedient when her mother had been in the school, cheeky and rebellious when she hadn't. Rosemary hadn't told Helen about all Jane's misbehaviour and had stopped doing so altogether after the occasion when she'd seen Jane, aged about 10, changing into her games kit. The back of her thighs had been covered in red stripes. Rosemary had assumed it was her father who'd been responsible for that.

*

Helen didn't shout 'I'm home!' when she entered the house. She assumed Jeremy was up in his study, and she needed to sit quietly with a cup of tea in order to regain some equilibrium.

She'd been dreading the conversation that she assumed Rosemary would have with her at school today, but she'd said nothing, indeed, had hardly spoken to her. Rosemary's near silence she'd found more upsetting than she would have if she'd been chastised about the events in her classroom yesterday. Then, even after Rosemary's entrance and her dismissal of the pupils, the only thing she'd said was to suggest that Helen tidy up the, and had then left her to get on with it.

Helen was unsure she'd be able to cope without Rosemary's friendship and support. She'd been prepared for hard work and got satisfaction from preparing her lessons, but being in charge of classes she was finding increasingly stressful. The older children were sometimes disobedient, and the ones in Year Six were cheeky, no, abusive, and sometimes disruptive. She found it hard to keep calm as she knew she ought; she often felt her gorge rising and resorted to shouting at them, something she knew was counterproductive. But she couldn't contain her anger. Yesterday, when that little devil Leila Bridges had screamed at her that she was a fuckin' old cow, she'd nearly lost it completely. But she wasn't going to hit her, was she? She was just threatening her. She wished she'd had the chance to explain that to Rosemary.

The cup of tea was calming her, but she felt the onset of an all-too familiar depression. Had Rosemary told Mrs Paton what had happened? Would this result in her changing her mind about the full-time post? Would that mean that the assessment for qualified teacher status would not take place? All Helen's dreams of a secure, less impoverished future were evaporating. But the real cause of her angst was her finally admitting to herself something about which she'd been in denial – that she wasn't cut out for teaching – no, more than that, she didn't enjoy teaching at all.

She heard Jeremy coming down the stairs and straightened herself from the hunched posture into which she'd slumped.

'Oh, I didn't hear you come in,' he said as he entered. 'Have you been home long?'

'A few minutes. I didn't want to disturb you if you were working.'

'D'you want a cup of – oh, I see you've got one.' She felt him staring at her. 'You must have been home more than a few minutes. Are you all right?'

'Yes, I'm okay. Tiring day at work.'

'I took the pizza out of the freezer this morning. I'll heat it up if you're ready to eat.'

'I don't want much to eat, but yes, go ahead.'

As Jeremy busied himself preparing the meal, Helen could only think of how the recent improvement in their relationship would be dashed if she were to give up her job. Now she was spending evenings preparing lessons, they were bickering less, and a kind of accord had developed between them, forged by their both being engaged in mindful work. Jeremy had become less distant, less dismissive of her concerns, since meeting that client of his in Aylesbury. He seemed to be finding the copy-editing venture he was engaged in to be more rewarding than writing novels, and he even passed some of his earnings over to her on the understanding that it was to be spent on household items, not on herself. Oh Lord, would all this go by the board if she were to become unemployed?

'How much of this do you want?' Jeremy asked as he brought the pizza to the table.

'Just a very small slice. Don't seem to have an appetite tonight. How are things going with Colonel Collinson's autobiography?'

Jeremy began to tell her as they began eating. He said he thought he'd cracked what the structure of the book would be, and Collinson was in general agreement with how it was panning out.

'Are you doing any more work on it tonight?' Helen asked.

'No, I think I deserve a break. I might go down to the *Bricklayers* to meet Jim for a drink.'

There was a lurch in Helen's guts. That meant she'd be by herself. By herself, but now unable to face lesson preparation. She wanted company. Jeremy now seemed to have the beginnings of a social life, but she was totally alone. She always had been. There was nobody whom she could call a friend apart from Rosemary, and their accord now seemed to be in the past.

As Jeremy began the washing up, she shocked herself by blurting out, 'D'you mind if I come to the pub with you?'

Jeremy wheeled round from the sink to face her. 'Oh, I don't think you'd enjoy it. Jim and I spend most of the time talking about writing. You'd be bored to tears. Anyway, don't you have lesson preparation to do?'

Helen could think of no answer to that.

'Oh, incidentally, did I tell you I'll be going to see Collinson again next week?'

'No, you didn't tell me. Is this going to be a regular thing?'

'Maybe. But I'll be away longer next week. Collinson's invited me for lunch.'

He turned back to the sink.

Helen couldn't remember the last time she'd been invited to join anyone for lunch, and resentment began to swell within her.

Chapter 10

'Come in, Albert! I'll put the kettle on. Tea?'

Jeremy immediately noticed that Eustace was wearing a collar and tie and what had obviously once been a smart suit. It made him feel uncomfortable, dressed as he was in his usual shabby gear. Was Eustace expecting another visitor, perhaps?

'Tea would be fine, Eustace.' He followed him into the kitchen.

He sat at the table and spread his typescript on the table while Eustace boiled the kettle. He seemed more hesitant in his movements than he had on Jeremy's first visit. When he carried the cups over, he spilled tea over the documents.

'I thought I'd email you my suggestions for your first three chapters, Eustace, so you'd have a chance to read them before you give me your comments.'

'Yes, I've read them. I noticed you haven't yet included any of my diary extracts.'

'No, we're nowhere near that stage in the story yet, are we? I wanted first to give an account of the character's upbringing. From what you've told me, I think that's what influenced your feelings towards the squaddies.'

'Do you think that's important?'

'Yes. The reader needs to have some hints about what has made a character the way he is.'

'Yes, I think I follow you, Albert.'

'Good. So, I suggest we go through what I've written page by page, and you let me know if I've written anything you disagree with. But just remember, Eustace, this isn't a pure autobiography; it's an autobiographical novel. That means that the main character, though based on you, is partly fictionalised. So I only need to know if anything I've written is totally at variance with the man that you were.'

'I see. At least I think I do. Shall we start?'

They began their discussion. There was little that Jeremy had written with which Eustace disagreed. Sometimes he said such things as 'My God, how did you know I felt like that?' At times he chuckled, and on several occasions joked about incidents in the chapters which were purely the product of Jeremy's imagination. Jeremy felt a growing regard for him.

They were about halfway through the chapters when Eustace said, 'D'you mind if we stop for a while? Alisa, my carer, will be coming soon with a meal, and I don't want her to think she's interrupting us.'

'Yes, that's fine by me, Eustace.'

'Let's go in the lounge. These chairs are hard on the backside after a while.'

Jeremy followed him into the lounge, noticing that he was unsteady on his feet even when using his walking-stick. The lounge was sparsely furnished, with a worn carpet and just two shabby easy chairs, one facing a television with a remarkably small screen. Eustace must have had it for years because it was the sort that was now never seen in shops. But the room was clean, and Jeremy found himself comparing it to the dust-covered surfaces of his own lounge.

Eustace sank into an armchair, and Jeremy sat down in the one opposite.

'Well now, Albert. You now have some idea of what my early life was like. I'd be interested to hear about yours. Tell me a bit about yourself. What was your father's job? What sort of school did you attend?'

'My father was an accountant. My mother died when I was twelve.'

'That must have been devastating for you. So was it left to your father to guide you through your teenage years?'

'If one can call it guidance, well, yes. I suppose so.'

'Tell me more.'

Jeremy wasn't sure that he wanted to. His teenage years were something he tried to forget. His father had been an austere, buttoned-up man who took little interest in his hobbies, nor his progress at school. There had been no intimacy in their relationship. But Eustace was inviting confidences, and it would be churlish not to give them.

'Let's just say that my father seemed to have no idea about the things that might concern an adolescent. He wasn't even interested in how I was getting on at school.'

'And how were things at school? Was it a comprehensive?'

'No, it was still a grammar school. All boys.'

'Did you enjoy being there?'

Jeremy hesitated, but decided there was no point in dissembling.

'To be honest, Eustace, no, I didn't. I suppose I was what you'd call a swot. I found it hard to make any friends because most of my classmates mocked those few of us who were interested in our studies.'

'Really? At a grammar school?'

'There were a lot of working-class pupils there. And many of the middle-class ones emulated them. They were interested in pop music, the fashions of the day, things like that. I suppose these days it would be called popular culture. And when they weren't talking about that, it was about the girls they went out with.'

'Did you have a girlfriend, Albert?'

'No. Never really got to know any girls. I knew I was unattractive. I was overweight, wore glasses. My classmates never let me forget the way I looked.'

'What about sport? Did you play rugby or cricket? Or maybe you preferred athletics?'

Jeremy laughed. 'No, I was hopeless at sport. That was another thing that set me apart. Many of my fellow swots were good at games.'

'So you were a bit of a loner, eh?'

'You can say that again. There were a couple of lads I got on with, but I never saw them outside school. I wanted to invite them home, but my father made it clear they wouldn't be welcome.'

'Y'know, Albert, what you've told me puts me in mind of how I felt when I couldn't relate to my squaddies.'

The same thought had occurred to Jeremy while he'd been talking. He was about to say it was a pity he and his classmates hadn't had a common enemy to unite against, such as Eustace and his squaddies had, but he decided this might sound disparaging. The last thing he wanted to do was to offend him.

'I assume you went into the Sixth Form?' said Eustace. 'Weren't things better for you then?'

Jeremy was about to reply when he heard a shout from the hall - 'Hello, Eustace? Where are you? I've brought you your lunch!'

'Ah, that's Alisa,' said Eustace. 'Let's continue this conversation while we're eating. I'm in the lounge, Alisa!' As he shouted this a smile broadened across his face.

Alisa served them their lunch in the dining room, a heated-up quiche. When she'd entered the lounge, Eustace had introduced Jeremy to her as his copy editor, and she'd made no comment other than 'Nice to meet you, Albert.' After Jeremy had replied in similar vein, she had disappeared, presumably to prepare the meal. Jeremy had a fleeting impression of a plump middle-aged woman with pleasant but unremarkable features.

'Bless you, Alisa,' Eustace said when she brought in the lunch.

'A pleasure, dear,' she replied, and briefly touched his shoulder before saying that she'd go and get on with a bit of clearing up.

'Does Alisa always prepare your meals, Eustace?'

'Good heavens, no. I asked her to do it today because I have a guest.'

Jeremy hadn't thought of himself as a guest, but maybe it was because Eustace had invited him for a meal that he was dressed so smartly?

Eustace attacked his quiche with vigour, some of it dropping off his fork onto the tablecloth. He seemed not to notice.

'Alisa always shops for me, though,' he continued. 'That's part of her duties. But I pay her a bit extra to do the cleaning; that's not a service her care company provides.'

'She seems very fond of you.'

'I don't know what I'd do without her. Apart from looking after me, it's good to have her company.' He took a sip of water from the glass next to him. 'Sorry I can't offer you beer or wine, Albert. I forgot to ask Alisa to get some. I can't touch alcohol, y'see. Not good to mix it with the drugs I'm on.'

Jeremy wondered if he should ask Eustace about the nature of his illness, but decided this might put a damper on the positive nature of their exchanges.

'Anyway, Albert, we were talking about you, weren't we? You were going to tell me about your time in the Sixth Form. Were you any happier there?'

'Well, more content. Most of the yobs had left. I began to immerse myself in my studies and got great satisfaction from it, particularly English Literature. But most of my classmates got even more involved in youth culture; you know, parties, discos, those sorts of things. That didn't appeal to me at all. So I decided to concentrate on getting good enough grades to go to university.'

'Ah, yes. I assumed you'd gone to university. Which one?'

'Manchester. To study English Literature, of course.'

'I imagine that was a liberation for you, eh?'

'Not entirely. You see – '

He was interrupted by the entry of Alisa. 'Finished your quiche, boys? No? I'll come back in a few minutes with your sweet, then.'

'This is delicious, Alisa,' said Eustace. 'Can't thank you enough. Sorry to have put you to the trouble. Hope I've not stopped you from doing whatever else you had planned for today.'

She began telling what her plans had been, and Jeremy noticed she spoke with a refined accent. It occurred to him that Eustace might be smartly dressed because of the extended nature of *her* visit rather than his. But as the two of them began talking, his thoughts turned to his time at Manchester. How much should he tell Eustace? If he told him everything, would he be demeaning himself? He wanted to retain the respect that Eustace seemed to have for him.

His thoughts were interrupted by Alisa leaving the room, saying she'd be back in a few minutes.

'So, Albert,' said Eustace. 'You were going to tell me about university.'

'Are you familiar with the term "culture shock", Eustace?'

'Yes. The term wasn't in use at the time, but I think that was what I experienced when I went to Northern Ireland.'

'Well, I experienced it when I went to university. I was the epitome of naivety. I hadn't realised that I'd be in a department where young women outnumbered the men. There was no avoiding them. Some were quiet and studious, kept themselves to themselves. But many were the complete opposite to the way I imagined students would be.'

'In what way?'

'Well, a lot of the time they spent talking about trivia, you know, clothes, popular music, the parties they'd been to, how much they'd drunk.'

'Not serious students, then?'

'Some of them could be. Those who spoke dismissively about men. They always spoke loudly so that any men around could hear them. They were convinced feminists, of course.'

'Ah, feminism. What were your feelings about that?'

'Well, I was intellectually sympathetic with women's fight for equality. I suppose that came from reading authors like Austen, Brontë, Woolf and Plath, oh, and Germain Greer, of course. But when I heard some of the women ranting, it seemed that I was an uncaring representative of a patriarchal society, responsible for female subjugation.'

The door opened, and Alisa came in carrying a tray which she placed at the side of the table.

'Ah, you've finished your quiche at last. You took your time, boys. Been nattering, have you?'

'Yes, we've been having an interesting conversation,' said Eustace. He peered at the tray. 'Oh, peaches and cream! My favourite! You're doing us proud, m'dear.'

'Nothing but the best for my favourite client. Take them off the tray, will you, so I can load your dirty dishes. When you've finished, leave things on the table for me to collect. You'll be going back to the lounge, I suppose.'

'Yes. Thank you again for all you've done, Alisa,' said Eustace, looking up at her with the smile he always seemed to have when talking to her.

'A pleasure, dear,' she said, and left the room.

Eustace gobbled his peaches and cream with relish, seeming not to notice, or perhaps not caring, that cream drooled from his mouth. Jeremy decided not to start talking lest Eustace felt obliged to reply, which might result in more drooling. So he began eating as well. As he did, he wondered where their conversation, when it resumed, might lead. So far, he'd found the experience cathartic, and he recalled Eustace's words at their first meeting – *I want to get it all off my chest!*

Eventually, satisfied grunts and the clatter of his spoon on the tabletop indicated that Eustace had finished his sweet.

'First rate!' he exclaimed. 'Right. Shall we adjourn to the lounge?'

Once settled in their armchairs, Jeremy asked Eustace for his comments on the chapters they had yet to discuss.

'Yes, in a minute, dear boy. But you hadn't finished telling me about your time at university. You were saying about the women there. I assume you gave them a wide berth?'

'As far as it was possible, yes.'

'But did you make friends there? What about the chaps?'

'Well, some of them I got on with. But I didn't see much of them. I was in digs, you see, a long way from the university, and when everyone moved into flats in the 2nd year, none of them asked me to share with them. So I didn't do any evening socialising. I didn't really want to. I gave up pretending I shared the average student's interests. So, I decided to emphasise my difference. I wanted to be seen as a man apart. I started dressing like someone from my grandfather's generation. Tweed jacket, neckerchief, flannel trousers. And a cloth cap when I was outside.'

'Still a loner, eh?'

'Not entirely. During the day I mixed with some of the more serious students in the department, including the women. In fact, one of them ...'

He hesitated.

'One of them what, Albert?'

'One of them I became friendly with. She was quiet and serious. I liked her because she was always interested in things I had to say. I got quite fond of her; it was like having a sister. Her religious beliefs were a bit outlandish, but she never tried to ram them down my throat. After finals were over, we went to a ...'

'Yes? Go on.'

'Well, after we left university, I married her.'

'Married? You're *married*?' There was no mistaking the look of amazement on Eustace's face.

'Yes. You sound surprised.'

'It's just that ... well, you don't give the impression of being a married man.'

'Well, I am. And we had a daughter.'

Eustace fell silent for a while. He covered his mouth with his hand and appeared to be deep in thought. Then his hand moved to his eyes, which he shielded for a few minutes.

'I hope you realise how lucky you are, Albert,' he said. 'I envy you having the comforts of a family. Much of my life I've spent alone. There's one thing to be said for being old and unwell – it's brought me the company of Alisa. Quite apart from her looking after me, she gives me the thing I've always craved.'

'What's that, Eustace?'

'Touch. You must have noticed how she touches my shoulder now and again? Touch means so much when you live alone. So, count your blessings, Albert, that you've got someone to touch you.'

It was Jeremy's turn to fall silent. Then he shook himself.

'Eustace, I'm sorry to have to hurry you, but we ought to get on with discussing your book. I've got a train to catch. I have a return ticket, you see.'

'Why do you depend on trains? It wouldn't be a long car journey from Watford to Aylesbury, would it?'

'I can't drive.'

'Really? You amaze me. Didn't you ever have lessons?'

'I started having them, but apparently I have a co-ordination problem. It used to worry me, but I don't care now because I can't afford a car anyway. Now, Eustace, can we make a start on your book?'

Jeremy very nearly missed his train. His goodbye to Eustace had been hurried. Alisa had been upstairs, so he'd had no chance to bid her farewell.

As he settled back in his seat, he recalled the contentment he'd felt after his first visit to Eustace. He wasn't quite so content now. On the one hand, he still relished the camaraderie that had developed between them and the prospect of further visits to him. And it had been a relief to offload his memories of a lonely childhood and adolescence. But while there was still a sense of empathy with Eustace, this wasn't quite as deep as it had been because he now felt .... what? Envy, he supposed.

This had resulted from Eustace's eulogising about the affectionate touching he received from Alisa. But compounding it was Eustace's assumption that as a married man, he would automatically have similar contact with his wife. Jeremy couldn't remember the last time he and Helen had ever touched each other with affection; in fact, they sometimes apologised to each other when accidental contact occurred. He'd grown accustomed to the sterility of their union until today. Now he was aware that something was missing from his life. But he knew that Helen would not be the one to provide it, and neither could he give it to her.

PART 3 - SUMMER

Chapter 11

Several weeks had passed since Jeremy's visit to Eustace Collinson. They'd had a few email exchanges and one telephone conversation about Jeremy's revisions to Eustace's manuscript, but Eustace had issued no invitation for Jeremy to make a further visit. Perhaps he wasn't well? Jeremy had noticed he was very breathless when he spoke on the phone.

Jeremy decided to concentrate on reading and copy-editing Stephanie Bridge's manuscripts. The grammar and syntax were still poor, the prose still abounded with clichés, there were frequent shifts from the viewpoint of one character to that of another, and sudden unheralded backstories. But for some reason he found her writing less trite than he had before. He had to admit that her descriptions of the appearance of her characters, in particular the way they dressed, were vivid. The plot and structure were also showing signs of inventiveness. The story started in the present, an account of the narrator's marriage, but soon launched into a series of backstories, but these were not sequential: they started in the recent past and worked backwards and forwards in time. He began to be intrigued.

Why had his opinion of her writing begun to change? Was it, he wondered, that because he was no longer writing a novel himself, he was becoming more engaged with the world outside his own literary comfort zone?

She never commented on the copy-edited versions of her manuscripts that he sent her, and he was beginning to find this frustrating. He needed to discuss her novel with her face-to-face. He wanted to discuss anything with anyone face-to-face, just to have the sort of contact that he'd had with Eustace, which he was missing. And to get away from the house. Helen was becoming increasingly withdrawn, and she seemed not to want to talk about her teaching at all.

He decided to email Stephanie.

Hello Stephanie. I think before we go any further with your novel, we need to have a discussion about where it's going. How would you feel about our meeting up so we can do this? Albert.

Her reply was almost instantaneous.

Hi Albert. What a coincidence! I was going to suggest the same thing. Let's talk about it. Here's my phone number. I'm okay to speak now. S.

Jeremy hurried down to the dining room, picked up the phone and punched in her number.

'Hi, Stephanie speaking. I assume that's you, Albert?'

'Yes. Hello, Stephanie.'

'So, you want to meet up? What exactly do you want talk about?'

Jeremy explained the value of face to-face contact and told her in some detail, that he had such discussions with another client.

'Yes, I'd like to meet you, Albert. If you're in front of me, I might get the chance to get a word in now and then.' This remark was followed by a throaty chuckle which had the effect of lessening the offence that Jeremy had started to take.

'Not only is discussion valuable, Stephanie, but there's a lot to be gained from listening to someone else read out loud what one has written. You see …'

'Oh, sorry, Albert. My son's just arrived. I've got to go. Can you phone me tomorrow evening?'

'Well, yes, but –'

'Bye, Albert.' The line went dead.

Jeremy was rather annoyed. An evening phone call was not what he wanted because Helen would be in the house. Their phone was in the dining room, and Helen objected to his taking the receiver up to his study, for some reason that she was unwilling to explain. He might have to pretend that he was talking to Eustace.

In the event, the next day Helen had a headache and retired to lay on the sofa in the lounge. He took the phone receiver up to his study.

But in their second telephone conversation, Jeremy was unable to address writing issues at all. Stephanie seemed more interested in asking him about himself: 'Where do you live?' 'How long have you lived there?' 'What sort of novels do you write?' 'Do you have a job other than writing?'

Reasonable questions, he thought, and answered them, but then: 'Are you married?' 'What's your wife's name?' 'Do you mind me asking how old you are?'

Why was she asking such irrelevant questions? He didn't want to offend her, so he answered them. But she continued her interrogation. 'Do you have many women clients?' 'Do you like female authors?' When she asked those questions, there was the hint of a giggle in her voice. He answered them honestly and was about to try to turn the discussion to more serious matters when Helen had called him from the lounge, and he had to tell Stephanie he'd phone her back the following day.

What sort of woman was she, he wondered? She didn't have a northern accent, and it was hard to gauge her age from her voice. Was she really serious about her writing, or was it just something she dabbled with in her spare time? But more important, he'd not had the chance to raise with her the matter of his expenses. Would she be willing to pay them?

Their third telephone encounter was the briefest. He decided to get straight to the point.

'Stephanie, you do realise I charge for my expenses? The rail fair to Leeds and back?'

'Yes, of course.'

'And there's my hotel bill. It'll be a long journey for me. I'll have to stay there overnight.'

'Oh, there's no need to stay in a hotel. I'll put you up here. I have a guest bedroom with en-suite facilities. And you'll find I can be a very accommodating hostess.'

There seemed to be no attempt to disguise the giggle when she said that.

Chapter 12

It was the first time Jeremy had been to the gents' outfitters in Watford. On the rare occasions he purchased clothes, he'd always gone to a store which sold mainly outdoor walking gear – it was always possible to buy cheap jackets and trousers in there which lasted him for years. He hadn't cared that they'd soon become shabby and threadbare. But now he needed to look smarter, and since Eustace Collinson had agreed to give him an advance fee payment, he could afford to do so. But he had a problem. He had no idea what he was looking for. A suit maybe? No, few men wore suits these days except when going to work in important offices. He tried to think what men wore when they were off duty, but he had no eye for current fashion, whatever current fashion was.

'Can I help you, sir?'

It was the young man whom Jeremy had noticed watching him as he hovered uncertainly in the entrance to the store. The lad was smartly dressed, though not in a suit, and he wasn't wearing a collar and tie, but one of those things without buttons that came up the neck and ended in a straight line. Ah, yes, hadn't Harold Fletcher worn one of those on occasions?

'Um, I'm looking for a jacket and trousers.'

'What sort of thing were you thinking of, sir, formal, or casual?'

'Well, casual, I suppose.'

'Casual tops and jeans are on the rails over there; the changing room's just behind them. Take all the time you need, and when you've decided what you want, bring them over to the cash desk.'

Jeans? *Jeans*? Jeremy had never worn them. He'd made a point of not doing so, even when at university. He walked over to the rail indicated by the young man. There were numerous denims hanging on it, but other trousers as well.

On inspecting them, they all had one feature in common – the legs were narrow. Jeremy liked his trousers to be roomy; the thought of being constricted didn't appeal to him. He turned to the rail on which jackets were hanging. But they weren't jackets. At least, not what he would have described as such. They had zipped fronts, were short, and didn't have lapels. He'd look an old fool wearing one of those.

Surely, the store must have blazers that one could wear with a collar and tie? And flannel trousers with creases? He couldn't see any. He'd better go and ask the young man, now seated at the cash desk.

But on his way over to the desk, he was seized again by uncertainty because he had no clear idea of what awaited him at his meeting next week. At first, he'd assumed it would be a semi-formal discussion such as he'd had with Eustace Collinson before the old boy had relaxed and opened up. But the three telephone conversations he'd had with Stephanie Bridges had taken them beyond the initial formalities, and she didn't seem to be the sort of woman who'd be impressed by a blazer, collar, and tie.

He made up his mind. He returned to the clothes rails. It took numerous trips between them and the changing room before he made his choice, a pair of blue needle-cord trousers and one of the few casual jackets that had buttons. Looking at himself in the mirror, he tried to convince himself that he didn't look too ridiculous, but what about a shirt? He couldn't wear a collar and tie under this outfit, and all his casual shirts were frayed. What sort of shirt should he have? Then he had an idea.

He took the jacket and trousers to the cash desk.

'Found what you want, sir?' said the young man.

'Yes. But before I pay, I'd like to buy a shirt.'

'Shirts are over there, sir. Do you have anything particular in mind?'

'Yes, one of those shirt things like the one you're wearing.'

'Oh, you mean a turtle-neck sweater. Yes, we have plenty of light-weight ones suitable for summer wear. They're over there. What's your chest size?'

Jeremy had no idea and had to submit to the indignity of being measured by the young man. He didn't like physical contact with strangers. He realised as the tape-measure was pulled round his torso, that this was the first time he'd been touched by anyone for years – no, decades.

He selected a light-blue sweater and returned with it to the cashpoint. The young man made no move to ring up the purchases but stood back and stared at Jeremy's feet. 'Do you have a pair of shoes suitable to wear with your needle-cords, sir?'

Jeremy now understood why he'd been uncertain about his appearance in the changing room mirror. His clumpy, scuffed brown shoes had just served to emphasise the narrowness of the needle-cord trousers.

'Can you suggest something?' he asked.

'A pair of dark blue trainers would be ideal to go with your cord jeans.'

'Jeans? But they're trousers!'

'Oh, no sir. The creases in them result from them hanging up for so long. They'll disappear soon after you've put them on.'

Ten minutes later, Jeremy left the shop with all his purchases in a carrier bag. Jeans and trainers! What was he thinking of? What had come over him? Why should he care what a client thought of his appearance? It was his literary expertise that he most wanted to impress her with, wasn't it? Or was it? He couldn't remember the last time he'd had this sense of pleasurable anticipation.

He decided to get a bus home because the carrier bag was too bulky to permit easy walking. It had been years since he'd been in the town centre, and he hoped the stop for his bus was where it always had been. He set off towards it, but progress was not easy. It was Saturday, and the streets were crowded not just with shoppers but by hordes of young people, some idling around, others charging about, whooping. Neither shoppers, idlers nor whoopers were inclined to make way for him. Many of them were apparently unaware of his existence as they shouted into their mobile phones or tapped on them, and those not shouting or tapping were engrossed in whatever they were listening to on their headphones. Jeremy abhorred the way mobile phones were reducing people's attention-span. He'd resolved never to buy one, but now, given the possibility of frequent calls to and from Stephanie Bridges, he wondered if one might prove to be useful.

His attention was so taken up with trying to avoid contact with his fellow pedestrians that he was suddenly shaken to hear a youngster shout to someone – 'He lives on Barclay Street, dun' 'e?' Barclay Street! Oh God, the name of the street he'd been trying to expunge from his memory for years. It was to Barclay Street that Jane had moved when she was 16 to lodge with the parents of a Sixth Form friend.

Jeremy had visited that house only once. Helen had refused to come with him. She'd said that Jane had made it plain that she never wanted to see either of them again. In vain, Jeremy had said that she was technically still a child and that they ought to demonstrate their parental responsibilities. So, he'd gone alone.

When he'd knocked on the door, it had been opened by a woman whom he assumed to be the mother of Jane's school friend. He'd explained that he was Jane's father and just wanted to check that she was okay. The woman had scowled at him and told him he'd got a bloody nerve, and that if he ever called again, she'd call the police, and they'd be interested to hear how he and that bitch of a wife of his had treated their daughter. Then she'd slammed the door in his face. Jeremy had been shaken. What had Jane told the woman? Surely she'd explained that it was he who'd always comforted her after Helen had doled out the punishments? But he'd known he'd be unwise to call there again.

Then, a year later, he and Helen had received a letter from the woman telling them that Jane had left to go to university and that there was no point in them trying to contact her. She was now 18 and had changed her name by deed poll. Attempts by Jeremy to persuade the police that she was a missing person had come to nothing.

'All in the past, all in the past,' he repeated to himself as he resumed his walk to the bus stop. He tried to convince himself he had a future now, a developing career, and the possibility of a new friendship. That led him to wonder how he could ensure that Helen wouldn't find the clothes he'd purchased. Even if she wasn't at home when he set out on his journey to Leeds, she might be when he returned, so he'd have to leave the house wearing his usual gear and carry his new clothes in a suitcase. That would mean having to change in the station toilets if he were to arrive at Stephanie Bridge's house looking presentable.

But once on board the bus, his thoughts returned, as he knew they would, to Jane. He *had* comforted her, of that he was certain.

Chapter 13

'Why do you need that big suitcase? You're only away for one night.'

'I'm having to take a pile of books with me. This client needs a lot of guidance, so I'm lending her some reading which she might find useful.'

'And why've you had your hair cut like that? It looks ridiculous.'

'I told you, didn't I? I was just getting tired of having to wash long hair.'

'But your head's shaved halfway up the sides; that's how some teenagers have it. It draws attention to your sticking-out ears.'

'I haven't got time to discuss all this again now. I've got a train to catch. Anyway, what are you still doing here? Why haven't you gone to school?'

'I told you why. There's been some timetable changes, and I won't be taking Year Six for a few weeks. My first class isn't till 11.'

'Look, I've got to go now. When I get to the bed and breakfast place, I'll phone you. I'll see you tomorrow evening.'

'All right. Goodbye.'

Helen sank onto a chair, put her elbows on the table, raised her hands, and placed her head between them. Oh God, if only she could sleep at night and not feel nauseous all the time. She wanted to cry, but tears wouldn't come. And if they were to, what would she be weeping about? She'd heard of women in unhappy marriages who couldn't wait for their partners to leave the house, those who welcomed the comfort of solitude. But then there were solitary folk who dreaded the prospect of another day spent by themselves, who longed for company, any company. Into which category did she fall? Both, she supposed.

She suspected that Jeremy was hiding something about his contact with his new female client in Leeds, but that merely annoyed her. She knew he was temperamentally incapable of having anything that could remotely be called an affair. But maybe they'd had a meeting of minds on the phone and were beginning a chaste literary liaison? And might this be so rewarding that he might want to go and live with her? Would she mind that? After all, the corpse of their marriage had long ago decomposed. But yes, she would mind because if she were also to lose her job, she'd be totally, utterly, completely alone, and the prospect terrified her.

Nothing had been said to her, either by Rosemary Massey or Mrs Paton, about her confrontation with Leila Bridges in the classroom two weeks previously. Rosemary was still distant with her, and Helen had noticed her giving her appraising glances. When she'd received a summons to Mrs Paton's office last week, she'd assumed it was because she'd been told of the incident, but it seemed she hadn't. The meeting was to inform her that because of a change in the timetable, she wouldn't be teaching Year Six for a few weeks. At the time, this had come as a relief, but now she wasn't so sure. It seemed too much of a coincidence.

Time to go. She should have washed her hair last night but couldn't summon up the energy. It was lank, and her grey roots were showing. The weather forecast was for hot weather, so she was wearing a rather skimpy dress purchased last month after she'd received her first increased salary payment. Glancing at herself in the hall mirror as she approached the front door, she wondered why she'd bothered. She hadn't the figure for it; her boobs were too big, her stomach bulged, and she knew her legs were shapeless tree-trunks. She looked as ridiculous as Jeremy with his new haircut.

Of course, it had to happen. When she stepped out of her door, there was Doreen Ellis walking down her garden path. Helen hadn't seen her since she'd started leaving early for work.

'Hello, Helen! I haven't seen you for ages. How are you? Hope you've got a raincoat with you. If there's a thunderstorm, you'll get soaked wearing clothes like that.'

'The forecast is for a fine day. I'm well, thank you. Now, if you'll excuse me, I'm in a hurry.'

'Oh, just hang on a sec. I've been wanting to ask you about your Jeremy for weeks. Our Kevin's told us that he doesn't teach his class anymore, and he hasn't seen him round the college at all. Has he left?'

'Yes, he's left. He's now self-employed.'

'That was a bit sudden, wasn't it? One week he was there, the next week he'd gone.'

'Well, you can tell your Kevin that Jeremy resigned. Now if you don't mind – '

'Seen anything of your daughter lately? Does she ever visit you? Never seen her around.'

Helen pushed past her without replying. Everyone was conspiring to plunge her more deeply into anxiety and depression. And now she was faced with a day at school where apparently nobody wanted to talk to her, not that she wanted to engage in staffroom chit-chat. She was going to be a bit late, which, in a way, was a good thing. She no longer liked being in the staffroom and preferred to go straight to her classes.

At least the kids in Year Five hadn't reached adolescence. She found them easier to control than Year Six – at least she used to. But since her confidence had started ebbing away, they'd started to be naughtier. Every remark and gesture made to her now seemed to be derogatory.

All classroom doors were supposed to remain open until the teacher was inside, but the door to Year Five's was shut. She entered to find few of the children were sitting at their desks; most were gathered round a boy who was holding something aloft. A noise was coming from it, thumping and wailing. The kids were clapping along to it.

'What have you got there?' she shouted. 'Whatever it is, turn it off and put it away!' The thumping, wailing and clapping continued. 'You heard me! Turn it off!' She felt her heart banging, almost in accompaniment, and a wave of nausea swept over her. Why wouldn't he listen to her? Why did nobody ever listen to her?

A girl, one of the few seated, was speaking to her. She couldn't make out what she was saying.

'What? Speak slowly, can't you?'

'It's Leroy's new iPad. It's gotta great sound, ennit? 'E's playin' YouTube, en'e?'

Leroy Myrie. One of the worst behaved kids in the class. He wasn't going to get away with this. She advanced towards him, nearly tripping over a chair leg.

'Leroy! Give me that! Now!'

He took no notice. Why did nobody take any notice of her? The little devil must have heard her, surely?

'Myrie! Give me that thing!' She had to scream. Had the clapping stopped? It may have, but the sound was still in her ears. And still Myrie ignored her. She made to grab the iPad, but he snatched it away. All she could now see was him; everything else in the room was misty. She saw him putting the iPad in his desk.

'Give it to me, at once!'

He said something, but she couldn't make out what. The mist surrounding her was now a fog. She tried to lift the desk lid, but his hands were pressed against it. She was suffused by an all-consuming rage, and then the fog overwhelmed her. She wasn't sure where she was. But she was sad, oh God, she was sad. Why wouldn't the good Lord help her? She burst into great gulping sobs.

*

'She's in no fit state to walk home, Rosemary,' said Mrs Paton. 'Would you mind giving her a lift? I'll get someone to cover your classes.'

'Yes, of course. I'll get her inside and stay until she's calmed down.'

'And when you judge the moment to be right, could you tell her that she's suspended until further notice? Disciplinary action may have to be taken, but there's no need to tell her that yet. I first need to find out exactly what happened and why.'

Rosemary collected Helen from Mrs Paton's office and escorted her to her car. Once inside, with a snuffling Helen sitting beside her, Rosemary battled with her conscience. Apparently, it had been Kathy Barnard who had entered the classroom to find Leroy Mylie lying on the floor and a weeping Helen standing over him. No doubt she'd taken great delight in quizzing the other pupils about what had happened and then reporting the incident to Mrs Paton.

Would all this have occurred, Rosemary wondered, if she'd taken Helen to task about her confrontation with Leila Bridges and maybe also informed Mrs Paton? She'd been distant with Helen afterwards as a means of showing her disapproval, but perhaps she ought instead to have counselled her. And now, she'd been burdened with the task of telling her that she was suspended from duties. At least, thank God, it seemed that Leroy Mylie had suffered no serious injury, but he'd had to be taken home by the caretaker.

She had to ask Helen repeatedly for directions to her house, but at last she drew up outside a modest semi-detached.

'Right, let's get you inside, Helen.'

No response.

'Helen! We're at your house! Let's get inside.'

Helen jumped as though she were hearing her for the first time. She fumbled two attempts to open the car door but eventually managed it and struggled to get out.

'You haven't undone your seat belt, Helen.'

Rosemary had to help her do that, but at last, they were standing outside the front door. More fumbling, this time with the door key, before Rosemary was able to follow her inside and into her kitchen. She was immediately taken aback by the untidiness of it – pots, pans, cutlery, food wrappings, crumbs and old newspapers covered every available surface. Then she noticed unwashed crockery piled in the sink. Didn't Helen's husband ever help with the clearing up?

Helen had sat down at the kitchen table. Her gaze was fixed on something in the middle distance. She was silent apart from the occasional sniffle. At least she was calmer than she had been. Rosemary considered trying to get her to talk about what had happened, but that would be to delay telling her what Mrs Paton had asked her to say. She sat down opposite her.

'Helen, I have something to tell you.'

There was no indication that she had been heard.

'Helen! Will you listen to me, please?'

Helen looked at Rosemary for the first time that day. Now they were in face-to-face contact, Rosemary was struck by how ill she looked. And old.

'Helen, I'm afraid I have to give you some bad news. After what happened this morning, Mrs Paton had no alternative but to suspend you from duties until further notice. That means you must not enter the school at all. Do you understand?'

'Does that mean I've been sacked?' There was no emotion in her voice as she said that. It was as though she were stating a fact rather than asking a question.

'No, it might not come to that. Mrs Paton will have to find out exactly what happened, and we'll need to hear your side of the story. Would it help you to tell me about it?'

Helen bowed her head and muttered something that Rosemary couldn't catch.

'Sorry, Helen, I didn't hear that.'

She then looked at Rosemary full in the face and said slowly and deliberately, 'I deserve to be punished for my sins.'

'Oh, I wouldn't call what you did a sin, Helen. Not good behaviour for a teacher certainly, but maybe you were provoked into losing your temper as you evidently did, and that's why – '

'You don't understand.' This was muttered. 'Nobody understands.' She rose from her chair and began pacing round the kitchen. 'It's the good Lord who's punishing me. I've asked for His forgiveness, but He won't give it. I only sinned once, and since then, I've tried to lead a godly life. But He will not let me forget it.'

She began snuffling again. Rosemary got up, went over to her and put her arm round her shoulder.

'Hush, my dear. Come on. Why don't you sit down and tell me all about it? Shall we go somewhere more comfortable?'

Helen pointed to a door across the corridor that led into the sitting room. Rosemary, still with her arm round her shoulder, led her towards it, wondering what the hell she was letting herself in for.

Rosemary would not describe herself as a religious person, but she was not an atheist. She had a vague notion that there might possibly be some sort of supreme being somewhere. But in times of trouble, she never sought solace from whomever or whatever that man, or woman, might be.

So she found it hard to understand the statements of remorse that came from Helen as she sat opposite her in the lounge. It was difficult to engage with her because what she said was couched in terminology akin to a sermon from a minister who'd permit no interruption. Apparently, the Bible was the hand of God, and Christ died to make certain the salvation of the elect, but she was no longer one of the elect because she'd committed a mortal sin, and her prayers for forgiveness hadn't been answered, and she was condemned to perpetual agony on earth which would continue when she was in Hell.

When at last she stopped, Rosemary ventured to ask her some questions.

'I take it you were brought up in a religious household?'

'Yes.'

'What sort of religious sect was it?'

'It's not a sect. We believe in the one true word of God. My parents instilled in me the need to be righteous, which I was, and I was comforted by God's guidance. I continued to follow God's word when I left home and went to university.'

'Helen, I must ask you this. What was the mortal sin you say you committed?'

Helen lowered her eyes and muttered, 'Jane was conceived in sin.'

'You mean you weren't married? Was the father the man who's now your husband? Jeremy's his name, isn't it?'

'Yes.'

'When did you become pregnant?'

'In my final year at university. I thought Jeremy was an upright, moral man. He wasn't like the other students who spent all their time drinking and fornicating. We became friends. But we went to a party to celebrate the end of finals, and he got drunk, and he insisted that I drank too, and … and Jane was conceived that evening.' She began to weep.

'But you got married, didn't you, and you've been married ever since. You've both raised a child. Surely that counts as atonement for what you call a sin?'

'No. It never can. Jeremy wasn't interested in helping me to raise Jane in the way she needed to be. It was left to me to try to instil in her the need to be godly. But she never obeyed me. That showed that God hadn't forgiven me.'

Rosemary could think of no way to try to convince her that she might be wrong. It would be like trying to persuade a vegan that there were some benefits that accrued from eating meat. She tried a different tack.

'But you and Jeremy have stayed together, haven't you? You must have brought each other some comfort?'

'This isn't a real marriage; how could it be? After Jane was born, I took a vow of chastity. We sleep separately. I thought this would bring God's forgiveness. But it hasn't.'

Rosemary decided to abandon her attempt to counsel Helen, and to concentrate instead on finding how she might cope with the next few days.

'What time does Jeremy come home, Helen?'

'He's not coming home tonight. He's away on business.'

'I don't like to think of you being by yourself tonight. Do you have a friend you can stay with?'

'No. I don't have any friends.'

'Right. Listen. You go and pack some overnight things. You're going to stay with me tonight.'

Rosemary was anticipating a rebuttal, but Helen just breathed, 'Oh, thank you,' and left the room, presumably to start packing. Left to herself, Rosemary could think of only two things. The first was how lucky she'd been to have enjoyed an active sex life with Martin right up to the time she was widowed. The second was a vision of the red stripes she'd seen on the back of Jane's thighs when she was a pupil at the school. At the time, she'd assumed only a man could be responsible for that. Now she wasn't so sure.

Chapter 14

The gents toilets at King's Cross station were just that: toilets. Jeremy had hoped such a facility at a main line station might contain a changing room, but no, just rows of urinals and about ten cubicles. There was no alternative but to use a cubicle. It was cramped, and it was a struggle to get his suitcase inside it. Once he'd managed that, the effort required to open it and take out his new clothes and put them on required the agility of a contortionist. While he was blundering about, a voice came from the next cubicle.

'Havin' it away with a bloke in there, are yer, mate?' Jeremy felt himself blushing. Not a good start to his expedition.

It was difficult fitting his old clothes in the suitcase because his boots were so large. When he finally managed it, he felt obliged to sit on the toilet seat to wait for the fellow in the next cubicle to finish his business, not wanting to encounter him on his way out. The process was taking him an age. When eventually mission was evidently accomplished, to the accompaniment of satisfied grunts, Jeremy decided to wait until after the toilet had been flushed and give the fellow time to wash his hands and leave.

At last, he thought it was safe to emerge. Getting his suitcase out of the cubicle was an effort because it now weighed much more, filled as it now was with his bulky old clothes and heavy boots. Was all this effort worth it, he wondered? What was he expecting of the forthcoming meeting? He had no clear vision of what might transpire. He'd not engaged in any fantasies. He just wanted to look presentable for a client who happened to be a well-spoken woman.

He inspected himself in the mirror in front of the washbasin. It was a short mirror, so he couldn't view his needlecords and trainers. But his casual jacket and turtle-necked sweater didn't look too bad. But, oh God, his haircut. Helen was right. It just emphasised his protruding ears. What had possessed him to have it cut, no, shaved, so short at the back and sides? It was, he knew, the assumption that the woman he was to meet probably mixed with men who were smarter and – what was the word? – ah, yes, *trendier* than he. But he'd only succeeded in making himself look grotesque. His rimless spectacles didn't help, but he couldn't afford to buy new ones.

He left the toilets and made his way to the entrance to Platform One. There was half an hour to wait before his train left. He'd left early to escape from Helen. Recently the composure which had resulted from her increased teaching hours had begun to evaporate; she was back to her old self, usually silent, sometimes giving vent to outbursts of rage, sometimes dissolving into tears. In fact, she was worse than she ever had been. He'd given up the attempt to find out what was troubling her since questioning her just resulted in silence.

But there was another reason for his early arrival. He wanted to savour some time on Platform One before his train departed. He had happy memories of Platform One. It was there he'd spent hours of his childhood armed with his Ian Allen guide, trainspotting. He'd had to travel from Luton to do that, but it was the one activity of which his father approved; apparently, he'd been a trainspotter himself back in the days of steam locomotives. Jeremy had wished he could have seen those, especially *Mallard*, but they had long passed by the time he took up the hobby.

He'd continued trainspotting well into his teenage years, long after his few school friends had abandoned the pastime in favour of the pursuit of girls. Girls had held no appeal for him. They were an alien species, and he didn't know what to say to them on the rare occasions he encountered them. Though he hadn't admitted it to himself at the time, they'd rather frightened him.

He walked along the platform, which was filling up with people. Its spaciousness was as he remembered, but that was all, because he'd had no interest in, or even awareness of, the buildings that lined its left-hand side, his attention always being focussed on reaching the far end of the platform where he'd stand for hours, gazing at the locomotives at the front of the carriages.

He walked to that same end and was heartened to see that there were what appeared to be trainspotters standing there, notebooks in hand. But they weren't children or teenagers. They were middle-aged or even older. And exclusively male, as indeed trainspotters always had been. That had been the other appeal of trainspotting – girls never did it.

'Passengers for the 12.30 train to Leeds are advised to board the train now, as doors will be closing in the next two minutes.' The disembodied voice jerked him back to the present.

Once on board and settled, he reached for his suitcase to extract the book wanted to read on the journey. But as soon as he opened the case, he knew he'd forgotten to pack it. He now had over two hours to do nothing but stare out of the widow and try not to think about the past nor to worry about what the day might bring.

Stephanie Bridges had given her address as a road in Headingley. The taxi from the station took him past Leeds University, then along a road adjacent to a tree-lined park, and then continued on past houses which grew in size as the journey progressed. It seemed the woman lived in a prosperous area. He thought this might be the case; her voice on the phone had not a trace of a northern accent, though he knew from his time in Manchester that such an accent was not necessarily an indication of deprivation, far from it. Some of his fellow students from the north had had far wealthier parents than he, not that this had stopped them from calling him a fuckin' posh southerner.

The taxi turned off the main road and drew up outside a house that was so large it could almost be described as a mansion. He paid the taxi driver, who'd called him 'luv' whenever he'd addressed him, clambered out and stood for a while adjusting his clothes. Why was he feeling so nervous?

Ten minutes later, he was sitting in an armchair in a spacious lounge waiting for Stephanie Bridges to enter with what she'd called refreshments. When she'd answered the door, his first impression was of a tall, slim woman, thin face heavily made up, black hair reaching down to her shoulders. How old? Hard to say, late 40s maybe? They'd shaken hands, and she'd asked him to follow her up the stairs to his room. While following her, he'd noticed she was wearing tight jeans.

She'd shown him into his room, indicated the door to the en-suite and had then said, 'I'll leave you to unpack, then. Have you eaten since you left home? No? Okay, the lounge is through the door on the left in the hall. Take a seat in there, and I'll bring us some refreshments. Leave the door ajar, please.'

He surveyed the room as he sat waiting. It was luxurious; a deep pile carpet, leather chairs, and a large drinks cabinet positioned next to what he assumed was a wood-burning fireplace. On the other side of the room was a bookcase, a big one. He was about to get up and inspect its contents to ascertain the nature of Stephanie's literary tastes but decided he didn't want her to come in and find him snooping. There was something slightly intimidating about her.

The door was pushed open, and she entered carrying a tray which she placed on a coffee table positioned in front of a settee. Then she stood facing him.

'Sorry I took so long, but I was getting so warm in my jeans I decided to change into a dress. Do you like it?'

Jeremy was taken aback. What a strange question to ask after such a short acquaintance!

'Oh, yes, very nice.' He assumed this to be an appropriate response.

'You don't think it's too short for a woman of my age? I've been told I still have the legs to get away with it.'

'Yes … I mean no … it's not too short.'

'Aren't you hot in that turtle-neck sweater? D'you want to go and change into something more comfortable?'

'Oh … no, I'm okay. I don't have anything else packed. I like to travel light.'

'Well, if you get too hot, you could always change into your pyjamas, assuming you've brought some. Oh, your face! I was joking, Albert!' She gave the throaty chuckle that Jeremy remembered from their phone conversations. He was discomforted. Was she really an aspiring author?

She sat down on the settee. 'I've made us a snack. Hope cheese and biscuits are okay. There's white wine to go with them and coffee to follow. Come and help yourself.'

Jeremy walked over to the coffee table, loaded one of the plates and made to carry it back to his chair.

'Oh, you won't be able to reach your wine glass over there. Come and sit here.' She patted the settee cushion next to her.

Jeremy didn't intend to have any wine, but it would have seemed churlish to return to his own chair. So he sat down next to her, taking care to avoid any contact with her body. He nibbled the cheese and biscuits, and because his mouth was full, he couldn't tell her to stop when she began pouring wine into the glass in front of him. She filled it to the brim.

'Now, Albert,' she said as she turned to face him. 'First things first. Do you mind if I call you Bertie? Albert doesn't suit you at all.'

Jeremy did mind, but he didn't feel able to rebuff her, partly because his mouth was still full. He shook his head. So far, she had made all the conversational running, and it had teetered on the brink of a flirtatiousness that was disturbing. He wanted to get down to the business of her writing, but that would have to wait until after this lunch because he'd left her manuscripts and his notes up in the bedroom.

'This is a wonderful house you have,' he said. 'Have you lived here long?'

'Since I got married. My husband ran a successful business. He died about ten years ago, just before we got divorced, thank God, otherwise it might have been left to one of his fancy women.'

'Oh, yes, I see – '

'But the upkeep's horrendous. Most of the rooms I've let out to students. Postgraduates, of course. Don't want youngsters rampaging around and messing up the furnishings. I just live in this wing. There are three bedrooms in it, mine, a double one for my son, Simon, when he comes to stay with his wife, and your en-suite. My bedroom's right next to yours, Bertie.'

As she said this, he was conscious of her staring at him. He found himself reaching for his wine glass and taking a swallow, anything to avoid having to look her in the eye. When, at last, he finished his cheese and biscuits, he stood up.

'Right, Stephanie, let's get down to business. I'll just go up and get the notes I've made on your manuscripts. Do you have a hard copy of them available to refer to?'

'Hard copy? What's that then?'

Jeremy explained. As he did so, he noticed she was grinning.

'Have you got a hard copy, Bertie?'

'Yes, it's upstairs.'

'Well, I'll show you mine if you show me yours.' She giggled. 'But don't bother with my manuscript yet. There are a few things I want to ask you first. Sit down and finish your wine.'

There was something about her manner that brooked no disobedience. Jeremy sat down again. She turned to face him.

'Bertie, before we go any further, I want to make sure that you're the right man to help me publish my novel. You've told me you've been doing this job for years, so you must have contact with lots of publishers. So, can you guarantee that you'll find me one? It's most important to me that it's published.'

'I'm afraid it's never certain that a novel will be published. But I can guarantee to help you make it publishable.'

'How will you do that, then?'

'What we really need to address is the way the novel seems to be structured. The way you're doing it is interesting, but the time-sequence is all over the place, and that would confuse a reader. And you – '

'It sounds like I've got a lot of work to do, then. Will you help me with all that?'

'Of course, that's what you're paying me for. But it's going to take a lot of time and email exchanges.'

'There's no need for emails, is there? Now we've got to know each other, you can come up here, and we can work on it together.'

'But that'll cost you, Stephanie. My travel expenses for one thing, and then there's – '

'Oh, I'm sure I can make it worth your while.'

With that remark, she placed her hand on his knee. Jeremy jumped to his feet.

'I'll go and fetch my notes.'

Up in his bedroom, Jeremy wondered whether he'd inadvertently entered an asylum, albeit one containing only one inmate. What on earth was the woman after? All those suggestive remarks and gestures! Yet despite those, she'd sounded serious and sincere when asking if he could guarantee that her novel would be published. Yes, of course, she'd feel that publication was important for her; didn't every writer?

He extracted her manuscript and his notes from his suitcase and made to go back downstairs but stopped. The prospect of them sitting together on the settee to discuss her writing wasn't inviting. She might seize the opportunity to make further body contact. Even if she were attractive, such intimacy would be anathema to him, but she wasn't. Close contact with her had revealed, under the heavy make-up, a deeply lined, almost wizened face. She looked as though she'd once been a heavy smoker.

And what in God's name did she see in him? He knew he'd never been attractive to women even as a young man, and now he was running to fat, his nose was peppered with red blotches, and his ears seemed to stick out even more now he had short hair. If the woman was sex-starved, couldn't she find a younger, fitter man to satisfy her? But maybe she had in mind the idea that her sexual favours might serve as a substitute for paying his expenses? He must make her aware that this wasn't an option. He picked up his documents and went downstairs.

In the lounge, she was sitting with her legs up on the settee, and her skirt had ridden up to mid-thigh.

'You took your time, Bertie. I was wondering if you'd decided to change into your pyjamas after all.'

'Stephanie, now that we're going to discuss your novel in detail, could we sit at a table? I'll need to make notes, you see, so I'll have to have all the documents spread out in front of me.'

The smile on her face vanished. 'Oh, really? Well, we'll have to go into the dining room if that's what you want.'

'Yes, it is.'

She pulled down the hem of her skirt, rose from the settee, and walked purposefully to the door.

It was a large, square dining-room table, so even though she sat at right-angles to him, there was a fair distance between them, and she showed no inclination to move closer. At last, he felt able to embark on what was the purpose of his visit.

He told her that at this stage, he wasn't concerned with grammar, syntax, and punctuation, though the problems with these would have to be addressed eventually. He told her she needed to restructure the entire novel and to avoid rapid changes of narrative viewpoint. He gave copious examples of these failings in her narrative. She seemed to be listening, but her gaze was fixed on her copy of the manuscript, and she gave no indication that she understood what he was saying.

When he finished his monologue, he waited for a response, but she remained silent. He decided to ask the question he'd sometimes put to members of the Rebel Writers group.

'Stephanie, let's imagine that I haven't read any of your manuscript. Pretend I'm a publisher or an agent. Give me a short summary of what your book's about. In other words, sell it to me.'

'It's about a family, isn't it?'

'But tell me more. What's the plotline? Who are the main characters? What's the climax to the story?'

She was silent for a moment, then said, 'It's too complicated to explain.'

'Well, let me put another point to you. You have numerous backstories in the novel, but these aren't sequential.'

'What d'you mean?'

'I'll give an example. Take the son of the woman who seems to be the main character. You obviously want to write about his history and how this affected her. But you don't start with how he was as a child or teenager. You write first about how he was a few years ago, then go back to when he was at university, and I think you've started writing about how he was before that. And the same device applies to the other characters. It's very disjointed and doesn't seem to be leading anywhere.'

'But's that's how you remember things, isn't it? You think about things in the recent past, then things that happened before that. At least, that's how I think.'

This was being hard work, Jeremy thought. 'Well, can you tell me how the story ends?'

'I've no idea. I just write what comes into my head and hope the story will work out somehow.'

Jeremy decided that to press the point would be to discourage her. He didn't want to do that; he needed her custom. He suggested that they take one character, one of the women in the novel, and together work out what her story might be. She agreed to do this, and they settled to the task. He managed to get her to contribute, and later, he was surprised to find, on glancing at his watch, that they'd been at it for nearly two hours.

'Would you like a break?' he asked her.

'I need more than a break. Sorry, I've got to go and relax in the lounge for a while.'

'Okay, Stephanie. While you're having a rest, I'll take a walk around the area. I noticed a pub near here when I was in the taxi – the *Skylark*, was it called? Does it do food? I need some supper.'

'Oh, you mean the *Skyrack*. You don't want to go there. It'll be full of students. There's a better place further up the Otley Road in Lawnswood. Bertie, d'you mind if I come with you? Don't feel like cooking tonight. After I've had a rest, I'll be fit to be seen with. And we can carry on talking about my writing when we're in the pub.'

She got up, placed a hand on his shoulder, then left the room.

Once in the pub, which was more like a restaurant with a bar, she showed no inclination to talk about her writing. She had insisted they go there by taxi, saying that she wouldn't be fit to drive home as she intended to make the most of an evening out by enjoying some wine. But at least she wasn't attempting to engage in flirtatious chat. She seemed to want to know more about his life, questioning him about his upbringing, his jobs, his wife, and whether they had children. He didn't want to talk about Helen or Jane, but wondered if reticence might speak louder than words, so he told her the bare minimum. Then she started to tell him about her own marriage, volunteering the information that she'd only stayed with her husband as long as she had because of his wealth and the fact that he'd been good in bed. She downed copious amounts of wine and kept topping up his own glass. When Jeremy got up to visit the toilet, he staggered and realised he was tipsy.

When he returned to the table, she was standing up.

'I've come over very tired, Bertie. I think bed calls. I've phoned for a taxi; it'll be here in a few minutes.'

'We haven't discussed your writing at all, have we?'

'Plenty of time for that tomorrow.'

'But I've got to leave early. I've booked a train for eleven o'clock.'

'Well, in that case, you'll have to come back and see me again soon, won't you? Come on, let's get outside so we don't miss the taxi.'

As they walked to the door, she took his arm. Once they were in the taxi, she took his hand. To have shaken it off would have been bad mannered, wouldn't it, and to his surprise, it felt rather comforting.

She paid the taxi driver and led the way to the front door. Once inside, she turned to him.

'I'm going straight to bed, Bertie. Are you staying up?'

'No, I'll probably go to bed myself – oh, God! Oh, Jesus!'

'What's the matter?'

'I've just remembered I promised to phone my wife this evening!'

'That's no problem, is it? Do it now.'

'I'll have to use your phone, Stephanie. Is that all right?'

'What's wrong with your mobile?'

'I don't have one.'

'That's amazing! You are the only person I know who doesn't. Yes, by all means use my phone. There's an extension in the lounge. I'm off up now. Goodnight, Bertie.'

He hurried into the lounge. It was 10.30. Helen would still be up. She never went to bed until after midnight because she said she found it impossible to get to sleep anyway. But how could he explain the lateness of his call? Ah yes, total immersion in his work with a demanding client.

He dialled his home number. No response. He tried again, nothing. What the hell was wrong with her? Was she deliberately ignoring his call because he was making it so late? He wished they had an answerphone so he could leave a message. He tried dialling once more. No reply. There was no alternative but to go to bed.

He climbed the stairs. There was no sound from Stephanie's bedroom; she was probably asleep already. He pushed open his bedroom door, took off his jacket and was sitting down to remove his trainers when he glanced over to his bed. There was someone in it.

'Hurry up, Bertie. It doesn't do to keep a lady waiting.'

Chapter 15

'I'll drop you at home on my way to school,' said Rosemary. 'Are you sure I can't tempt you to some breakfast? You didn't eat anything last night either. You need to keep your strength up, Helen.'

'I don't think I could keep anything down. The biscuit I had with my cup of tea was enough.'

'Well, if you're sure. I'd better go and get a few things together. Will you be ready to go in about fifteen minutes?'

'Yes, I've got my stuff packed ready. Rosemary, I'm so grateful to you for letting me stay the night. I couldn't have faced being alone in the house.'

'Don't mention it, my dear. It's the least I could do.'

Rosemary knew that in fact, she'd done very little. The previous evening, she'd tried to engage Helen in conversation about all sorts of matters other than her present situation – books, music, TV programmes, even current affairs – but her responses had been monosyllabic, though at least she'd stopped weeping. Her whole body had been tense, and though she looked exhausted, she gave no indication that she wanted to sleep. In the end, Rosemary had suggested she take a sleeping pill – she had a packet stored away for those occasions when she herself had had a particularly trying day – and Helen had assented. But Rosemary had to feed it to her as though she were a child, to the extent of holding the glass of water to her mouth to encourage her to swallow it.

The night's sleep had obviously done her some good; this morning, she was at least able to talk in coherent sentences. But oh, what a pathetic creature she looked! Dishevelled clothes, hair awry, face pallid and lined, eyes bloodshot: she appeared much older than her 50 years. She reminded Rosemary of those poor souls she sometimes encountered sitting begging in the town centre. How on earth would she be able to cope with whatever arose from yesterday's events?

At least today she was able to get into the car unaided and remembered to fasten the seat belt.

'How are you going to spend your day, dear?'

'Housework, I suppose.'

'When's your husband due back?'

'Early afternoon, I think. Oh Lord!'

'What's the matter?'

'He was going to phone me yesterday when he arrived in Leeds, but he didn't. Suppose he phoned last night when I was at your place?'

'Well, can't you say you were out with a friend?'

'Haven't got any friends.'

Rosemary took her hand off the steering wheel and touched her arm briefly. 'Oh, yes you have, Helen. I'll be here for you if you need me.'

After she'd dropped Helen at her door, Rosemary sped off towards the school. She was on the verge of being late, something she prided herself on never doing. She went straight to her first class.

By break time, she was dying for a coffee and hurried to the staffroom. When she entered, she saw most of her colleagues grouped round Kathy Barnard. She was, as usual, obviously enjoying being the centre of attention. Rosemary was about to collect her coffee with the intention of taking it to a seat as far away from her as possible, when her attention was seized by what she was saying.

'... so, Mrs Paton had to leave her office when the copper said he wanted to talk to me alone. She didn't look pleased about that, I can tell you. Anyway, the copper asked me what I'd seen when I went into that Johnson woman's classroom. So I told him. He was writing down everything I said in a notebook. Then he asked me if I had any idea what had happened before I went in, so I told him I'd asked the kids in the class and that they'd said Johnson had hit Leroy Myrie round the head and knocked him over.'

'What did the copper say about that?' asked Bill Bentley, one of the younger teachers.

'Nothing. He just kept on writing it down. He was a very young fella, good looking too. I wouldn't mind being arrested by him; he could put me in an arm-lock any time.'

'Get on with it, Kathy,' said Bill. 'What happened next?'

'He asked me if I'd heard anything about Johnson behaving like that before. I told him she was well-known for shouting at the kids and losing her temper. Well, ever since she'd started being in charge of classes.'

Throughout this interchange Rosemary stood, conflicted between shock, pity, and anger. Oh God, the police were involved! Could things get any worse for poor Helen? And that little bitch, Kathy Barnard, telling the police about Helen losing her temper! Rosemary's anger was so intense she felt like marching over and shouting insults at her, and a slap round the face might do *her* some good.

Then the woman fell silent. Rosemary turned and saw that Mrs Paton had entered and was scanning the room. Her glance fell on Rosemary.

'Ah, Mrs Massey, could I trouble you for a moment of your time? Please come along to my office.'

There was no offer of coffee on this occasion, and Rosemary wasn't even invited to sit down. Mrs Paton remained standing, her face screwed into an expression that Rosemary couldn't fathom.

'Rosemary, I assume you know something of what's happened, as you were present when Miss Barnard was relishing telling everyone all about it.'

'I heard a bit of it. Oh, Jennifer, how awful that it should have come to this.'

'You don't know the half of it. I'm not even sure that I do. The policeman arrived just before the school opened, asking to speak to me. Apparently, Leroy Myrie's father has made a complaint about his son being assaulted by one of our teachers, and did I know anything about it? I said I was aware there'd been an incident, but I hadn't witnessed it. I told him that I'd suspended the teacher in question with immediate effect. Oh, Rosemary, please sit down. I'm sorry. I'm so upset that I'm forgetting my manners.'

Rosemary sat down, expecting Mrs Paton to join her, but she went over to the small fridge and opened it. 'I need something to buck me up,' she said, and pulled from it a bottle of tonic water and then the bottle of gin which Rosemary knew was in there. She showed no sign of shame at revealing it and poured a sizeable measure into a coffee cup.

'I'm not a boozer, Rosemary, I keep this gin for one of the governors who likes a snifter. Would you like some?'

'Not for me, thanks.' Rosemary's drinking was restricted to a small glass of sherry before supper. She wasn't convinced by her boss's explanation for the presence of gin in the fridge.

Mrs Paton sat down and took a swig from her cup.

'Anyway, the policeman asked to speak to the member of staff who witnessed the incident, said he believed her name was Miss Barnard. I suppose he got that information from Leroy or his parents. I went to fetch her from her class, and when we got back to my office, the policeman told me he wanted to speak to her alone. I didn't want to go to the staffroom, so I sat on that chair along the corridor. What was I thinking of? I should have gone to supervise Kathy Barnard's class.'

'It's quite understandable that you'd forget to do that, Jennifer.'

'Kathy Barnard was in there with him for what seemed like ages. When she came out, she didn't seem surprised to see me sitting in the corridor. She looked horribly smug and told me the policeman would see me now, just as though I was some minion.'

She took another swig of gin.

'When I got back in, the policeman told me that some of the children in the class would be interviewed about what had happened, in the presence of their parents. He then said that I'd be contacted about the result of the enquiry and that

I might be called as a witness if the case went to court. And Helen must be barred from entering the school. That was his parting shot.'

'Oh, poor Helen!'

'Never mind Helen, what about the school? If all this gets to the papers, think what it'll do to its reputation, and to mine! I've spent the past four years making this an institution to be proud of. This could ruin my career prospects.'

Rosemary felt a sudden urge to leave Mrs Paton to wallow in her own concerns. She got up to go, and as she did, she saw another measure of gin being poured into her boss's cup.

Chapter 16

'Are you awake, Bertie?'

'Yes.'

Jeremy was conscious of her head turning towards his on the pillow. He was unable to face her.

'Would you like a cup of tea in bed?'

'No thanks.'

'Are you sure? I'm going to make one for myself.'

'I'm going to get up. Don't want to miss my train.'

'Oh, well, let me get up first then. I'll go down and get some breakfast ready.'

'Okay, thanks.'

He kept his eyes closed as she rose from the bed, assuming she was naked.

'I'll give you a shout when it's ready.' A pause, then – 'Bertie! Look at me!'

He opened his eyes. Thank God, she'd put on a dressing gown.

'No regrets, I hope, Bertie?'

He was unable to reply.

'I hope not, because I haven't. See you downstairs, then.'

As soon as she left the room, Jeremy got up. He grabbed his pyjamas from the floor. Last night, Stephanie had thrown them there after she'd frantically pulled them from him.

'No regrets?' she'd asked. He didn't know. In fact, he hardly knew who he was; certainly not the Jeremy Johnson who'd entered the bedroom some eight hours earlier. It was as almost as though he'd lost his virginity, and in a sense, he almost had, for he'd been celibate since the evening Jane had been conceived. Back then, he had experienced the triumph that he assumed all young man felt after their first time. He didn't feel triumphant now, though some of the feeling of release that had surged through him once Stephanie had rolled off him was still there.

He'd hardly slept at all after that, because the release had been tinged with guilt. Why? Given the nature of his chaste relationship with Helen, it wasn't as if what had happened could be described as unfaithfulness, could it?

He entered the shower-room, grateful that he wasn't required to walk pyjama-clad along the corridor to a separate bathroom, possibly to run into a still-rampant Stephanie. The facility was well appointed, luxurious even, and he spent a long time under the shower, taking care to thoroughly cleanse his private parts.

Then, as he dried himself on an exquisitely soft towel, the reason for his guilt came to him. He *had* been unfaithful, hadn't he? Unfaithful to his life of the mind, the life to which he'd sworn allegiance when he'd started to write. He'd made that oath to avoid falling into temptation, for on the one occasion he'd succumbed, it had resulted in his having to abandon his anticipated career in academia. He had resolved that no woman would ever again divert him from the path of literary righteousness. Had Stephanie done that? Would he still be able to concentrate on his copy-editing career? He told himself that for her it was probably just one of many one-night stands, and that he would eventually be able to put the events of the previous night behind him.

He washed and shaved, brushed his teeth, and while dressing he wondered if his attempt to be stylishly clad had been taken by Stephanie as an indication of his wish to be more than just her copy-editor. No, that was ridiculous. His clothes and haircut just served to emphasise his physical imperfections.

He went downstairs to the dining room.

The table, covered in a patterned cloth, was laden with a variety of breakfast cereals, a toast-rack, a toaster, pots of marmalade, fruit, a jug of milk and a cafetiere filled with coffee. Jeremy couldn't help but contrast the scene with the scruffy wasteland of his breakfast table at home.

Stephanie appeared at the door. 'Help yourself to cereals, or fruit if you'd prefer. Would you like a cooked breakfast to follow?'

'No thanks.'

'And I can brew some tea if you don't want coffee.'

'No, coffee's fine.'

Because they were talking at a distance, Jeremy was able to appraise her. She was dressed in jeans and a tee-shirt which suited her trim figure, but her face looked old, lined, and not very attractive. He was comforted by that.

She sat down next to him, and they began eating. They exchanged the occasional remark, and to his relief, she made no mention of the previous night's events. After the cereals had been eaten, she stood to insert bread into the toaster, then turned to face him.

'Well, Bertie, how do you find Leeds compares with Manchester?'

'Why should I be able to make a comparison?'

'But you were at Manchester University, weren't you?'

'How did you know that?'

'It's on your LinkedIn profile, isn't it?'

Good God, what else was on his profile that was irrelevant to the enhancement of his career? He'd written the profile when he'd first joined LinkedIn because the site seemed to invite such revelations. He would eliminate such information as soon as he got home.

But Stephanie hadn't finished her interrogation.

'Was it at Manchester where you met your wife?'

Jeremy didn't answer and decided it was time to leave. Mention of his wife reminded him that there'd been no answer to his phone call last night. He must call her as soon as possible, but not from Stephanie's phone. To contact one's wife from a house where one had slept with the householder would reek of the action of an unprincipled roué. He stood up.

'I'm sorry, Stephanie, but I don't have time to finish breakfast. I need to get off.'

'But your train doesn't go for hours!'

'I know, but I have some shopping to do, and it's best to get it done in town before I catch the train. I'd better go up and pack my things.'

'Oh, what a pity. I was hoping …' she was saying as he left the room.

Upstairs, he packed hurriedly, wondering what might be the nature of their parting. How did one bid farewell to a woman with whom one had been intimate, yet with whom one was supposed to have a professional relationship? What would she expect of him – a hug, maybe? Or even a kiss? What would that signify? He'd noticed that these days everybody seemed to hug and kiss on greeting and parting, but he had never done it, and it had never been done to him.

He lugged his suitcase downstairs. She was standing in the hall by the front door, mobile phone in hand.

'I've phoned for a taxi, Bertie, but before you go, can I make one thing clear?'

'Yes, what's that?'

'I'm deadly serious about getting my novel published, and I do hope that what happened last night hasn't made you want to stop advising me. I listened to what you said yesterday about the novel's structure, and I'll email my first revised efforts to you as soon as I can.'

'Yes, I'll continue helping you, Stephanie.'

She advanced to stand less than a foot away from him.

'I'm so glad about that. When you've received my offering, I hope you'll visit me again so we can discuss it face-to-face. And if you want it to be a chaste visit, I'll go along with that, reluctantly, I might add.'

Jeremy had no idea how to reply to that. He wanted her custom and didn't want to offend her by rejecting what was an offer of further intimacy. He remained silent.

'Bertie, I want to ask you one more thing. Why don't you have a photo of yourself on your LinkedIn message board?'

'I don't think it's necessary for my clients to know what I look like, that's all.'

'But I'd like something to remind me of you.' With that, she lifted her mobile phone and held it to her face.

'What are you doing?'

'I'm taking some shots of you. Okay, that's done. Well, I suppose it's time to say goodbye. Put your suitcase down for a minute, Bertie.'

Jeremy was so taken aback by being photographed that he complied. She stepped forward, put her arms round him, pressed her loins against his, nuzzled his neck, then kissed him.

'Goodbye, Bertie. We'll have a professional relationship, I promise, but we can still be fuck-buddies, can't we? No strings, just a bit of fun.'

Jeremy picked up his suitcase. 'Goodbye, Stephanie.' She made no move to open the front door, so he did it himself. The taxi hadn't arrived, so he resigned himself to waiting for it on the pavement. But he moved many yards away from the entrance to Stephanie's garden.

When he arrived at Leeds station, he had nearly an hour to wait before his train left. The vast concourse resembled a shopping centre, so at least he could browse in a bookshop and have a much-needed coffee. His hurried departure from Stephanie's house had been made before the cafetière had been poured. But first, he must call Helen.

But where were the public phone booths? He made a tour of the concourse but couldn't see any. Had they fallen victim to the curse of the ubiquitous mobile phone? He joined one of the long queues to the ticket offices, and when at last he reached a service window, he was told that they were situated on a distant part of the concourse to which he was given directions.

Once inside the booth, he was surprised to find that the machine took coins; he'd been expecting, it being the 21st century, to have to use a credit card. Coins at the ready, he dialled his home number. It rang for a long time, but there was no reply. What the hell was Helen doing? It was Saturday, so she wouldn't be at work. Out shopping, maybe? No, she never did that until after lunch. He replaced the receiver, worrying that something untoward might have happened; she'd been in a depressed state when he'd left her. Oh God, if she became so ill as to prevent her working, they'd sink even deeper into poverty.

He returned to the main concourse and entered the book shop. But it wasn't what it claimed to be. There were no books. The shelves were filled exclusively with magazines appealing to every low-life hobby it was possible to imagine. Many of them were encased in plastic wrappers to prevent them being opened, and it was easy to imagine what they contained.

There was nothing else to do but have a coffee while he waited for a train. Sitting nursing a plastic cup in a crowded Costa, he wondered how, without a book to read, he could divert his thoughts away from both Stephanie and Helen during the long journey home. He was beginning to have some regrets about abandoning his novel-writing in favour of copy editing. Although writing could be a lonely and introverted activity, at least when engaged in it he became immersed in the characters of his imagination, those who would think and behave the way he wanted them to, unlike Helen and Stephanie.

Stephanie. Maybe he should try to stop thinking of her as that and revert to Ms Bridges? There had been a sociology lecturer at the FE college who refused to refer to the prime minister as 'Boris' because, he said, the use of the Christian name conferred on the bastard a likeability that was totally at variance with the loathsome man he was. But Stephanie couldn't be described as loathsome, could she? Did he like her? She seemed to like him; after all, she'd said they could be 'fuck-buddies'.

Jeremy had winced when she'd used that term. He had heard it used before and had associated it with those who saw sex as a mere pastime, those who eschewed such virtues as commitment and who were no doubt devotees of the plastic-wrapped magazines he'd seen in the so-called bookshop. But, thinking about it now, was it perhaps the use of the expletive 'fuck', now so common in everyday speech, that had offended him? And if so, why? After all, D.H

Lawrence had used it in 'Lady Chatterley'. If you analysed the term 'fuck-buddy', it simply meant 'friends who had sex'. Is that all that Stephanie had meant by it? Could its definition be expanded to mean also 'professional associates who had sex'?

Jeremy was proud of the fact that many of the characters in his two unpublished novels were conflicted individuals. He was now one himself. Part of him wished to remain the celibate professional literatus that he had been up until yesterday. But there was now a wish to experience again the sensation of release he'd felt the previous night.

Something else troubled him slightly about Stephanie – and yes, he would continue to think of her by that name. Why had she questioned him so much about his past, his jobs, his wife? Her questions had been framed almost as though she wanted him to confirm things she already knew.

The eleven a.m. train to London Kings Cross will depart from platform six in ten minutes.

He picked up his suitcase and hurried off, aware that he'd probably spend the entire journey thinking about Stephanie and worrying about Helen. But once on board the train, suitcase stowed on the luggage rack and ticket in hand ready to be checked by the conductor, he fell asleep almost immediately.

***

Stephanie stood at the front door as Bertie walked down her garden path, hoping he'd turn to wave her goodbye, but he didn't, and as soon as he reached the pavement, he walked away. She went back to the dining room, sat down and poured herself a coffee. The table still contained much of the breakfast that Bertie hadn't eaten in his evident haste to leave.

His visit had been a success. She'd learned more about his past, and it seemed to confirm what she'd suspected. Most important, she now had his photograph on her mobile phone. But what a strange fellow he was! Confident to the point of arrogance when talking about her writing and how it might be improved, but seemingly unable to engage in casual chat, let alone flirtation. And he was naïve to the extent of being totally innocent when in bed with her. It had been like seducing a virgin, though when it came to the climax he seemed to enjoy it, but afterwards, he'd seemed reluctant to engage further intimacies, even spoken ones.

But her main objective had been achieved. He would continue to visit her, of this, she was certain, and the time would surely come when she could set up a meeting between him and Simon and Jessica. And another benefit would come from his visits. She would re-write her novel, in fact, make it a totally different story. What had started as a casual hobby would now require total commitment, for it would be based on the life of Simon and Jess. She would love to see Bertie's reaction when he read the later chapters.

She drained her coffee cup and decided to phone Simon before he left for work. Jessica always left for work first.

She dialled his number, and the call was picked up immediately.

'Hello?'

'Hello, Simon, it's Mum. How are you?'

'I'm okay. And you?'

'I'm fine. I've got some news for you. Is Jess around?'

'No, she's gone shopping.'

'Listen. He came yesterday and stayed overnight. I found out a lot more about him.'

'You're talking about that Albert Rennie, fellow, I suppose?'

'Well, that's what he calls himself. But more important, I took a photo of him on my mobile.'

'For God's sake, Mum. You know I don't want to involve Jess in all this. What's the point of digging up her past? She's come to terms with it.'

'So, you say, Simon, but I think- '

'Sorry, Mum, I don't want to discuss it now. In any case, Jess is due back any minute.'

'But Simon – '

'Oh, leave it, can't you? I need time to give this a lot of thought. Got to go now. Bye, Mum.'

The line went dead.

Stephanie wasn't too disappointed. Simon's reaction had been much as she'd suspected it would be. She was resigned to it being a long haul.

Chapter 17

Jeremy was woken by the jerk of the carriage as the train pulled up at Kings Cross. Despite having dozed for most of the journey, he felt exhausted and weak; when he reached to pull his suitcase from the luggage rack, he was overcome by dizziness and almost keeled over. As he staggered onto the platform, nearly stumbling over in the process, he remembered that he was still dressed in his going-away outfit. The thought of visiting the gents to go through the process of changing back into his every-day gear was like anticipating the exertion required to engage in doing press-ups. He couldn't face it. Maybe, if he felt better, he could change in the toilets at Watford station. Oh, why the hell should he bother? If Helen questioned his attire, he could always say he purchased it in Leeds with the cash payment made by his client.

But he needed to visit the toilet. Once inside, he entered a cubicle as it was necessary to remove his incontinence pad before peeing. As he did so, he noticed it was quite dry. Not even damp. It was the first time a pad had been dry since he'd started wearing them. Was this, he wondered, the result of last night's activity? A reason, perhaps, to continue his relationship with Stephanie? He was still mulling this over as he made his way to the underground station.

But the tube journey from Kings Cross to Baker Street was excruciating. What was wrong with him? Okay, he wasn't the fittest of men, but on the rare occasions he'd previously been to London, he'd never had trouble balancing when getting on and off escalators, nor when strap-hanging on the packed tube. Why was it so crowded on a Saturday afternoon? Looking at his casually dressed, noisy fellow passengers, most of them youthful, he concluded they were all pleasure-seekers.

At Baker Street, he was relieved to find seats available on Metropolitan Line train out to Watford. Of course, the pleasure-seekers wouldn't be travelling in this direction until late at night, would they? He sank back in his seat. The distance now between him and Stephanie hadn't led to disenchantment, but his thoughts were now entirely with Helen, with what sort of mood she'd be in when he got home. He hoped to God she'd snapped out of the depressed state in which he'd left her, so he could give her a piece of his mind for not answering his phone calls.

'Anyone in?' he shouted as he closed the front door behind him.

Silence.

He dumped his suitcase in the hall and went through to the kitchen. He'd assumed he'd find the usual array of crumbs, unwashed crockery and cutlery on the table, and the sink full of similar items, but there was no evidence of any eating having taken place at all. Then his shoe crunched against something on the floor – it was a broken glass. Why hadn't she picked that up and disposed of it?

'Helen!' he shouted. 'Where are you?'

No response. He went through to the living room and found the television was on but with the sound turned down. A chat show was being broadcast, but there was no Helen sitting watching it. Had she been called to go somewhere urgently and, in her haste, forgotten to turn it off? But where, and by whom, could she have been summoned? There was nobody else he knew of who might want to see her.

A sense of unease enveloped him. He climbed the stairs. Her bedroom door was shut as was always the case when she was inside. She never allowed him in there. Hesitantly, he tapped on the door. Nothing. He banged on it. The resulting silence was unnerving. He decided to risk her wrath and pushed the door open.

She was there on the bed laying on her back, fully clothed. Her eyelids were fluttering.

'Helen, are you all right? Why are you up here?'

Her eyes opened but didn't focus on him. 'Feeling ill,' she muttered, 'trying to get some sleep.'

It was then he noticed the open packet of paracetamol on her bedside table.

'Helen,' he said, waving the packet in front of her face. 'How many of these have you taken?'

'Not many.' Her speech was slurred. 'Just trying to gessome sleep.'

'When was the last time you ate something?'

'Can't remember.'

'Can I get you anything?'

'No.'

He bent over her. It was the first time in years that they'd been in such close contact.

'Helen, listen. Is there something that's troubling you?'

Tears began welling from her eyes, and sobs soon followed. Now was the time when a husband would take a wife in his arms, give her some comfort. But he couldn't. It would be like embracing a complete stranger. In any case, she would shrink from him if he were to try.

'I'll bring you up a cup of tea and a biscuit,' he said. 'Maybe you'll be tempted when they're in front of you.' It was relief that he made his escape from her room.

Something must have happened, he said to himself as he searched the cupboards for the packet of teabags. If she wasn't going to tell him, how on earth could he help her? And would she want it? He suspected she might need professional help. He'd become accustomed to her occasional bouts of depression alternating with outbursts of rage, but her condition now spoke of some sort of mental breakdown.

He abandoned his search for biscuits and was about to brew the tea when the telephone rang. He went into the hall to answer it.

'Hello? Am I speaking to Mr Johnson?' It was a mature female voice.

'Who's speaking, please?'

'My name's Rosemary Massey. I'm one of Helen's colleagues.'

'Yes, I've heard Helen speak of you. How may I help you?'

'I've been trying to phone Helen all day, but there's been no answer. Is she there? Can I speak to her?'

'I'm afraid she can't come to the phone at the moment. She's in bed, not feeling too well.'

There was a momentary silence down the line, then –

'Do you mind my asking what's the matter with her?'

'I wish I knew. She hasn't eaten, says she feels ill, and is rather … well, emotional.'

'Mr Johnson, I believe you've been away since yesterday morning, am I right?'

'Yes, and I've only just got back from Leeds. I was visiting a client and – '

'So Helen hasn't told you anything about what happened at school on Thursday?'

'No, she doesn't seem to want to talk at all. Why, what did happen?'

'It's not something I want to speak about over the phone. Would you mind if I came over now to see Helen? I might be able to help her.'

'I'd be very glad if you would, Mrs Massey.'

'Good. I'll be there in about fifteen minutes. You'll tell her I'm coming?'

'Yes, I'm sure she'll be pleased.'

'I'll see you soon then. Goodbye, Mr Johnson.'

'Goodbye.'

Jeremy replaced the receiver and almost ran up the stairs to tell Helen the news. He received a smile in return. Well, as he'd told Mrs Massey, she was obviously pleased. But not half as delighted as he was. Someone else would be taking the weight from his shoulders. But what, he wondered, had happened at the school on Thursday?

***

Rosemary had to steel herself to ring Helen's front doorbell. Was she doing the right thing to get further involved in this situation? She'd told Helen she was her friend who'd always be there for her. But all sorts of other potential problems might arise from her visit, not least how much, if anything, she should tell Helen's husband.

The front door was opened. The man standing in front of her was, well, 'undistinguished' was the word that came to mind.

'Mrs Massey?' he asked.

'Yes. Please call me Rosemary.'

'And I'm Jeremy. Come in.'

No sooner was she in the hall when he said, 'What was it that happened at the school that's so upset Helen?'

'Oh, Mr … Jeremy, I'd like to see Helen first, if you wouldn't mind. I want to see what state of mind she's in.'

'Yes, I see. Well, I'll be in the kitchen when you're ready to speak to me, if you want to speak to me, that is. Helen's bedroom is the door on the left on the landing.' He turned and walked away.

That's a good start, thought Rosemary, *I seem to have offended him already.* She climbed the stairs, tapped on the door, and opened it immediately.

Helen was on the bed, curled in a foetal position. She seemed unaware that anyone had entered.

Rosemary approached her, bent over her head and said quietly, 'Helen, are you awake? It's me, Rosemary.'

The head jerked, then turned to face her. *Oh Lord, she looks like death.* There was no sign of recognition. 'It's Rosemary, dear. Sorry if I've woken you.'

Her eyes widened, then suddenly she turned on her back and struggled into a seated position. 'Rosemary? Oh, Rosemary! How lovely to see you!'

Rosemary sat down on the bed beside her. 'I've come to see if I can help you in any way, dear.'

Helen made no reply but shifted to be close to her. Rosemary placed a hand on her arm. Helen's response to that was to fling her arms round Rosemary's shoulders and to bury her face in her neck. Rosemary tentatively embraced her, and this resulted in an outburst of sobbing.

When at last she was a little calmer, Rosemary disentangled herself from their embrace and took her hand.

'What's troubling you, Helen?' she asked. 'Has something happened since I left you here yesterday morning?'

'No! It's just … just …. I was alone all day, then all night. Couldn't stop thinking about what's happened. Couldn't sleep. Worried about how I'd tell Jeremy. Didn't want him to come home. Don't want to be with him.'

'Well, my dear, he's got to know soon, hasn't he? What will you tell him on Monday when he sees you're not going to work?'

'Don't know! I've got to spend all tonight and all tomorrow thinking about it! I've prayed for guidance, but the Lord doesn't answer me!'

Rosemary felt that she herself would benefit from divine inspiration, for she had no idea how to advise her. She found she was unable to look Helen in the face.

'Rosemary, could I …'

'Could I what, Helen?

'Could I come and stay with you again tonight? And tomorrow as well? I felt so much better when I was with you. And I wouldn't have to speak to Jeremy.'

'Oh, Helen, I don't think that would be a good idea.'

'Why? You told me you were my friend! You said you'd always be here for me, didn't you? Why aren't you looking at me?'

Rosemary knew she was unable to tell Helen the reason she couldn't give her sanctuary, that she'd be a possible witness in a criminal case.

'Helen, have you eaten anything today?'

'What? No. Why?'

'I think you need something inside you. I'm going to make you a cup of tea, or coffee if you prefer. What would you like to eat?'

'Nothing!'

'Well, I'll go and see what you've got in your cupboards to see if there's anything you might fancy. Maybe Jeremy can advise me about that. I'll bring it up here and we can carry on talking.'

She got up from the bed.

'Rosemary, don't leave me, please!'

'I'll only be a few minutes, dear.'

'Are you there, Jeremy?'

'I'm in the kitchen.'

She entered. He was sitting at the table, doing nothing, staring into space.

'Well, how did you find her?'

'She's obviously unwell, and I don't mean physically. Jeremy, have you ever considered she might need professional counselling for her mental state?'

'Of course I have! But she won't take any advice from me. Anyway, are you going to tell me what happened at the school on Thursday?'

'She had a bit of a breakdown. The head's advised her not to attend for a while.'

'For how long? Will she continue to get paid?'

'I've no idea. Look, Jeremy, I think she needs some sustenance. Does she like tea? Is there anything for her to eat that might appeal to her?'

'Not really. Stocks are running low. She hasn't done any shopping. You might find some sweet biscuits in the cupboard. Yes, she drinks tea.'

'I'll take some up to her. I need to carry on talking to her.'

'Well, while you're doing that I'll go to the shops and get some ready meals in. I've hardly eaten myself today. I'll be some time; you might be gone when I get back.'

I hope to God I am, thought Rosemary.

'Right, I'm off. Best of luck with Helen.'

'Goodbye, Jeremy.' *Nice to meet you too*, she thought.

She made the tea, managed to find a half-empty packet of biscuits, and carried them upstairs. She was relieved to

124

see that Helen was still sitting up, gazing vacantly across the room. For the first time, Rosemary took in her surroundings. The bedroom was sparsely furnished; apart from the single bed there was only a dressing table and chair, no pictures were hung on the walls, and the whole room could do with a lick of paint. The floorboards were bare and needed dusting.

'Here you are, Helen. There isn't much here, but you need to eat. And a cup of tea. Can you get up? I need somewhere to put the plate and cup on.'

'Put them on the dressing table.'

She dragged herself from the bed, tottered over to the dressing table and sat down, having first moved the chair so it didn't face the mirror. She took a sip of tea then nibbled at a biscuit.

'Helen, listen to me. You need professional help with your problems. I think you'd benefit from counselling, by a psychiatrist maybe. Would you like me to try and arrange that?'

'No point. He couldn't help.'

'How do you know that?'

'If the good Lord won't forgive me, then I'm condemned.'

'Oh, Helen, what can I say or do to help you if you won't listen to me?'

She took a gulp of tea and swallowed hard. 'There is something you can do. Let me come and stay with you so at least I'm not alone. Why don't you want me to?'

Rosemary knew she'd now have to make the excuse that had come to her when she'd been downstairs.

'Well, you see, Helen, I have a gentleman friend staying with me for a while.'

'So you're a sinner too?'

It was time to go, Rosemary decided. Apart from getting her to eat and drink she'd been no comfort to Helen at all, for she seemed beyond any further help that she was able to offer.

'I've got to go now, Helen. But one thing I can do. If you feel desperate, or just want to talk, phone me any time. Here's my number'.

Helen took the card without a word of thanks.

Once outside, Rosemary heaved a sigh of relief and considered the lie she'd told Helen about a gentleman friend. For the first time since Martin had died, she rather wished she'd been telling the truth.

Chapter 18

Sunday had passed with excruciating slowness. Helen had hardly spoken to him at all. She had spent most of her time in her bedroom, only coming down to make phone calls to Rosemary Massey. It was on these occasions that she'd spoken to him – 'Go somewhere else, I want to call Rosemary' – and it was relief that he'd felt able to go to his study, freed from the obligation to remain downstairs on the alert in case she had another crisis that might demand his attention, though he'd had no idea of what possible help he could give her.

She had even rejected his offer to take refreshments up to her room, insisting again, when she eventually came downstairs to get something to eat, that he return to his study. When up there, he'd considered engaging in copy-editing, but that would have been akin to fiddling while Rome burned. But he knew his was not the concern of a loving husband for a sick wife, rather that of a weary hospital doctor who had a duty to attend to the welfare of the stranger on the ward.

He woke the next morning, surprised that he'd managed to have slept reasonably well – too well, in fact, for glancing at his watch he saw it was after eight o'clock. He dressed hurriedly, and on reaching the landing, he paused to listen at Helen's door. He thought he heard sounds of movement. Did that mean she might be getting up? Might even be coming down for breakfast?

He lingered over his cereals, coffee and toast, remembering the repast that had confronted him on Stephanie's breakfast table. It was the first time he'd thought of Stephanie for what seemed like days. As he ate, he wondered how the hell he was going to spend his day trapped in the role of carer. There were no further signs of life from upstairs. Maybe he should go up to ask how she was?

He was saved from having to make the decision by the door-bell ringing. He wiped his mouth, adjusted his track-suit bottoms, and went out to the hallway. On opening the door, he was confronted by a man and woman, both smartly dressed.

'Mr Johnson?' asked the man.

'If you're selling something, I'm not interested.' He started closing the door.

'We are police officers.   Here is my identification,' the man said, holding up a card. The woman also produced a card. Jeremy peered at them. It seemed they were Detective Sergeant Arthur Bingham and Detective Constable Linda Ferguson. He opened the door fully.

'We wish to speak to a Mrs Helen Johnson,' said Bingham. 'I take it you are Mr Johnson?'

'Yes. What do you want with her?'

'Can we come in, Mr Johnson?' said Ferguson. 'This isn't a matter we can discuss on the doorstep.'

Jeremy let them into the hallway, all sorts of implausible scenarios flashing through his mind.

'My wife's in her bedroom. She's not well.'

'Is she well enough to come downstairs?' asked Ferguson.

'I'll ask her. What shall I say this is about?'

'That's something we can only tell her ourselves, Mr Johnson,' said Ferguson. 'She would be well advised to co-operate, so would you please ask her to come down.'

This was said so assertively that Jeremy had no alternative but to comply. He went upstairs and entered Helen's bedroom without knocking. She was sitting on her bed. It took him some time to explain what was happening, and he wasn't sure if she understood, for she said nothing. But he held the door open and insisted that she come with him. She followed him down the stairs.

Bingham and Ferguson were still standing in the hallway. Jeremy asked them if they'd like to come into the sitting room but was told that wouldn't be necessary.

Bingham adopted an upright posture. 'You are Mrs Helen Johnson?' he asked.

Helen nodded.

'Please speak up, Mrs Johnson.'

A whispered 'yes' came from Helen. Jeremy was suddenly aware that this was a situation where he should be holding her hand.

'We are police officers, Mrs Johnson. I am Detective Sergeant Bingham, and this is Detective Constable Ferguson. We're investigating a complaint that you assaulted one of your pupils, Leroy Myrie. Is there anything you'd like to say about it?'

Helen gave a faint whimper and just stood staring at Bingham. Jeremy was aghast. Surely there must be some mistake? He stood, speechless.

'You have nothing to say, Mrs Johnson?'

Her response was another whimper.

'Mrs Johnson, I am arresting you on suspicion of committing that assault. You do not have to say anything, but it may harm your defence if you do not mention when questioned something you may rely on in court. Anything you say may be used in evidence. We will now take you to the police station for questioning. You may be there some time. If you are on any medication, you would be advised to bring it with you. Do you understand what I'm saying?'

Helen continued to whimper, but Jeremy found his voice.

'You must be making a mistake! Can't you see she's in no state to be taken into custody? I want legal representation, now!'

'Mr Johnson, please calm down' – this from Constable Ferguson – 'Your wife will be entitled to legal representation when she is being questioned. Now' – she took hold of Helen's arm – 'come with us, Mrs Johnson.'

'I want to come with her!'

'That's not possible, Mr Johnson,' said Bingham.

He took hold of Helen's other arm, and she was taken outside. Jeremy followed, and as she was led to a police car, she began to wail.

He ran towards her, shouting, 'Helen! It'll be all right!' He barged in front of them and stood between them and the car.

'Mr Johnson,' said Bingham, 'please return to your house now, otherwise I shall have to arrest you for obstructing police officers in the course of their duties.'

A hand was placed on Helen's head, and she was guided into the back seat of the police car. Ferguson got in next to her and Bingham drove the car away, but not soon enough to prevent Jeremy from hearing Helen continue to wail.

Dazed, he walked back to his house, but noticed Doreen Ellis was standing gawping at her front door. He hurried past her before she could speak, entered his house – the door had been left open – went straight into the living room, and collapsed in his armchair.

All that was in his head were images of the events that had just taken place, that and the sound of Helen wailing. He sat slumped in the chair for a long time.

Eventually, he rose to his feet. He began pacing the room, willing himself to try to think rationally.

Might she have done it? It was a distinct possibility; after all, she'd used physical punishment on Jane, but that wasn't really an attack. It was a measured response to misbehaviour. But what about her assaults on him? There was nothing measured about those; she'd been in a frenzy. Might she have been in a similar frame of mind when she assaulted that kid? But surely, she would never have behaved that way at work?

He was alone. There was nobody in whom he could confide. Might Helen be detained overnight? Would she be given nightwear and toiletries? Maybe he should get together things that she might need. He ran upstairs and entered her bedroom, though he had little idea what sort of things he was looking for. What would already be available to her in a police cell? He decided to search the drawers of her dressing table for items to take to her. He was just about to open a drawer, when he noticed a small card on the table surface. He picked it up. On it was written Rosemary Massey's name, address and telephone number.

Well, she couldn't be called a friend, but she was someone he could confide in about Helen. He went downstairs to phone her. There was no reply. *Blast, she's at work, isn't she?*

***

Custody Officer Bullock took charge of Helen when she arrived at the police station. She was wailing. Sergeant Bingham told him this was how she had been throughout the journey in the police car.

'Take her into the interview room, Constable Ferguson, and you'd better stay with us while I book her in.'

Linda Ferguson led Helen into the room and told her to sit down at the table. She didn't comply. Ferguson had to gently push her onto the chair. She stopped wailing, but sat with her head in her hands.

Bullock entered, sat down at the other side of the table, and indicated to Ferguson that she should sit beside him.

'Mrs Johnson, can you confirm that you know why you've been arrested and the nature of the charge against you?'

There was no reply: she kept her head in her hands and began crying.

'Mrs Johnson, you do understand that – '

'I'm a sinner!' This was screamed. She made to rise from her chair. Ferguson got up and gently eased her back, then sat down beside her. Bullock raised his eyebrows. Ferguson responded by shrugging her shoulders.

'Mrs Johnson, are you taking any medication?'

The prisoner's only response to this was to clench her fists and shake them against her temples. Bullock repeated the question, to no avail. He tried a different question.

'Mrs Johnson, you are entitled to legal representation at this interview. Would you like me to contact the duty solicitor?'

'Only God can be my witness!'

Bullock got up and beckoned to Ferguson. 'You'd better stay with her, Linda,' he muttered to her. 'By a stroke of luck, Macpherson's here. I'll get him to come and assess her. And I'll call the duty solicitor. He thinks he's bloody God anyway, so she might listen to him.'

He left the interview room and sought out the police surgeon, Dr Ferguson, who was in the canteen. In cases like Mrs Johnson's, Bullock sometimes suspected that the prisoner might be feigning mental illness. He gave Macpherson a brief account of the arrest and the way Johnson had reacted to it, then retired to his own office to have a much-needed cup of coffee.

He'd been in his office for half an hour before Macpherson joined him.

'I won't sit down,' he said. 'What I have to say won't take long.' His voice bore the trace of a faint Scottish burr.

'Well, Doctor,' said Bullock, 'what did you make of her?'

'She's in a fragile mental state, as I'm sure you realise. She was unable to articulate any coherent response to the questions I asked her.'

'Did she say anything about what happened when the alleged assault took place?'

'Oh come on, Sergeant, you know it's not my place to ask her that. My role is simply that of assessing a prisoner's health.'

'Is she having a nervous breakdown? Is she fit to be interviewed?'

'The term nervous breakdown is widely used and often inappropriately, I believe. I'm not a psychiatrist, and so I can't make a precise diagnosis of her condition. So I'm unable to advise you as to her fitness to plead. I shall, however, say this. Should you decide to charge her, she's in no condition to remain in a police cell. She requires careful observation and possible medication. I would suggest that if it's decided to charge her, she is released on police bail. I think her condition is such that she doesn't constitute a danger to anyone, except perhaps to herself.'

'Is there anything else we need to know?'

'No, there's nothing more I can tell you. I have an urgent case to attend to, so you'll forgive me if I take my leave of you. Good afternoon.'

***

Jeremy could settle to nothing. Reading or writing would be an impossibility. He had left a message on Rosemary's answerphone, but there had been no reply. What was happening to Helen? How long would she be kept in custody? Would the police inform him if she were to be detained overnight?

He paced up and down, kitchen to living room to dining room, then up to his study, then into Helen's bedroom, then into his own, but just standing staring at nothing wherever he found himself. He considered doing some housework – the place certainly needed it – but that activity would seem to sow the seeds of a possible future, a future without Helen in the house to do it. To think that he always welcomed her absence, indeed, relished the times when she was out! The realisation struck him that although their marriage was not a happy one and that though she'd become almost a stranger, there was sometimes a degree of comfort to be had from the occasional presence of someone else in the house.

The phone rang. *Rosemary already?* It was only just after four. He picked it up.

'Hello, Rosemary? I didn't expect – '

'Hello, is that Mr Johnson? This is Constable Ferguson.'

'Yes, what's happened? Is Helen all right?'

'Mr Johnson, this is to let you know that your wife is being released on police bail pending a possible hearing at the magistrates' court. Will you come and collect her from the police station please?'

'What? You mean she's been charged? And no, I can't come and pick her up. I don't have a car.'

'Oh. Well, in that case, you'll have to come by taxi. I want to explain to her again, in your presence, the conditions attaching to the bail.'

'But what's she been charged with?'

'I'd prefer not to discuss this over the phone, Mr Johnson. Everything will be explained when you get here. Good afternoon.'

'But – '

The line had gone dead.

Chapter 19

Jeremy was seized by the need to urinate. On relieving himself, he'd discovered that his incontinence pad was damp – no, more than damp, it was soaked. The easing of his problem that had resulted from Stephanie's ministrations had evidently ended. But he didn't care; he had more pressing matters to worry him. He was not just worried. He was angry, angry about the way the police had behaved. He'd been brought up by his father to believe that the constabulary were conscientious protectors of the law-abiding, but recent cases of police misbehaviour had made him begin to doubt this. Why weren't they concentrating on keeping yobs off the streets instead of pursuing misdemeanours mistakenly committed by respectable people?

He was approaching the phone to call for a taxi when it rang. He jumped – oh God, what now?

It was Rosemary Massey.

'Sorry, I wasn't home to take your call, Jeremy. I've only just got back from school.'

'Oh, never mind about that. Listen. Helen's been arrested. She's in police custody.'

There was a moment's silence, then, 'Oh my God! I suppose this is to do with her hitting … '

'What? You mean you know about that? All you told me before was that she'd had some sort of breakdown. Why the hell didn't you tell me she'd hit someone?'

'I know you must be upset, Jeremy, but please try to stay calm. Yes, I knew about the incident in the classroom, but I didn't know she was going to be arrested.'

'Well, she has been. The police took her away this morning. I think she's been charged.'

'Is she going to be detained overnight?'

'No. I've got to go and collect her. When I get her home, could you come round? She's so much calmer when you're here.'

'I'm not sure I can do that, Jeremy.'

'Why the hell not?'

'Because I might be called as a witness, and from what the headmistress has told me, I don't think Helen will be allowed to be in contact with anyone from the school, even though – '

'Witness? *Witness*? But good God, if it came to it, you'd be a witness for the defence, wouldn't you?'

'Please listen to me, Jeremy. Wait until you get Helen home. Phone me then. I'd like to help, but I need time to think about my position before I decide whether I can come over.'

'Your position? What about Helen's position?'

'I'm going to hang up now, Jeremy. But phone me later as soon as Helen's home. And do try to stay calm for her sake.'

Jeremy was left holding the receiver. He was overcome by a feeling of desolation.

When he arrived at the police station, he was directed to a side room. Helen was sitting in it, and Constable Ferguson was standing beside her.

'Mr Johnson,' said the constable, 'I need to repeat in front of you what Mrs Johnson has already been told. This is because she is very uncommunicative, and I want to make sure she understands what's been said.'

Jeremy's eyes hadn't left Helen. She was sitting hunched, making no eye contact with him, and her gaze was traversing the room as though she were trying to work out where she was.

'Mrs Johnson has been charged with the assault of a minor. She said nothing in her defence beyond saying repeatedly that she couldn't remember what happened. The evidence has been submitted to the DPP to make a decision on whether to continue the procedure given her possible mental state at the time of the assault. If the case proceeds, she will appear before a magistrate to answer the charge.'

'When will that be?'

'Hard to say. It could take up to a month. But it's the conditions attached to the police bail that I want to emphasise. She must make no contact with anyone connected to the case as this would be regarded as interference with a witness. She should remain in the house as far as is possible, and if she intends leaving for any reason, we must be informed in advance where she is going and why. She has been told all this, but I think you need to explain it to her again until you're sure she understands.'

'Yes, I'll do that.'

'Good. You may now take her home, but before you go, let me say this. This is off the record. The police surgeon has indicated that your wife would benefit from counselling, perhaps by a psychiatrist, because of her mental state. I suggest you take her to her G.P. and ask for a referral. Whatever transpires from that might help her defence if the case comes to trial. Good afternoon.'

Jeremy took Helen's arm and led her out. He had no idea what to say to her while waiting for a taxi, and when it eventually arrived, the journey was undertaken in silence.

When at last they were home, he said, 'Can I get you anything, Helen? A cup of tea perhaps?'

'Yes.'

'Let's get you into the living room.' He took her arm, led her there, and settled her in an armchair. It was akin to helping an old woman suffering from dementia.

When he handed her the cup of tea, she said, 'Thank you', and looked at him for the first time.

'I'll be back with you in a minute. I just want to make a phone call.'

***

Rosemary had made up her mind. It was what Jeremy had said on the phone that had convinced her even though he'd been rude to the point of offensiveness when saying it. What an arrogant, ill-mannered man he could be! Poor Helen, living with him must be hell. She had enough problems without having to cope with him. What, Rosemary wondered, was his attitude to her religious beliefs? She doubted that he showed much tolerance for them. Then she remembered how Helen had told her that she'd taken a vow of chastity following her daughter's conception. At the time, Rosemary hadn't considered how this might be for Jeremy. How had he coped with that? Maybe he sought satisfaction elsewhere? Even if he did, she could hardly blame him. For the first time, she felt a degree of sympathy for him. What a tragic couple they were. But maybe the recent events might serve to bring them closer together? Perhaps by giving support and comfort to Helen, she might also be helping Jeremy.

When she received Jeremy's phone call informing her that the police had left, she immediately set out on the short journey which had now become familiar to her. She parked outside the Johnsons' house, and the front door was opened before she had the chance to ring the bell.

'So, you decided to come, then. Helen's in the lounge. Before we join her, is there anything you need to tell me first? Have you thought about what I said on the phone?'

'Yes, I have, but Jeremy, don't you think it would be better to involve Helen in our conversation? I think she needs to interact with as many people as possible.'

'But she seems unable to take anything in; it would be – '

'Look, we should both be present. You can't keep her cooped up in isolation. That would just make her worse. It would be like being back in custody.'

'Oh. Okay, come in, then.'

Rosemary didn't know what to expect. Her thoughts returned to the last time she'd been with Helen in the lounge when she'd hysterically delivered her religious rant. She wasn't prepared for the sight of a shrivel-faced old woman sitting hunched in an armchair staring down at her clenched hands.

'Helen, here's Rosemary come to see you,' said Jeremy. He spoke slowly and loudly as if she were deaf or senile or both.

Helen raised her head. Her face was expressionless; there was no sign that she'd taken in what Jeremy had said. Rosemary dragged a chair over, sat beside her and took her hand, which remained clenched.

'Helen! Hello, dear! It's me, Rosemary.'

Her head turned. 'Oh, Rosemary.' This was said as though she were simply stating a fact. There was no indication of pleasure, nor even surprise.

'Helen, dear, listen to me. I know you've had a terrible time. But things will be all right, I promise you. This nightmare won't last long because I can help you.'

'No one can help me.'

'Helen, you do understand that in a few weeks you may have to appear in a magistrate's court?'

A nod.

'And that you'll have to plead guilty or not guilty to a charge of assaulting Leroy Myrie?'

Another nod.

'And how will you plead, Helen?'

'I don't know. I can't remember what happened.'

'Listen, dear. If your case comes to court, I will speak as a character witness. That means I'll say how long I've known you, tell the court that what you did was completely out of character and was the result of the great stress you've been suffering recently. You'll be found not guilty, I'm sure. Do you understand?'

There was a whispered, 'Yes.'

'I'll be back to see you tomorrow. And term ends on Friday, so I'll be able to come and visit you frequently over the holiday. But I've got to go now, dear. Everything will be all right, I promise.'

She kissed Helen's cheek and stood up.

Out in the hall, Jeremy told Rosemary he'd keep repeating what she'd said to Helen because he was still unsure she'd fully grasped it.

'Jeremy, I'm not sure what I told Helen will actually happen. But one thing I am certain of – I can't be called as a prosecution witness because I didn't witness the assault. But one thing worries me a bit.'

'What's that?'

'As a member of the school staff, I'm not sure I'm supposed to have contact with Helen. Certainly, it would be most unwise for her to visit me at home. But I will come to see her once the holiday starts. Nobody round here knows who I am, but if they ask you, you could always say I'm a social worker.'

'That's a good idea. Yes, come and see her. I've got a lot of work to catch up with. I need the money, and in any case, I'm not cut out for being a carer.'

As she got in her car, Rosemary began once again to revise her opinion of Jeremy.

Chapter 20

Nearly two weeks had passed since Helen's return home, and there was still no indication of whether she'd be brought to trial. The first week had been hell for Jeremy. Rosemary's visits had been infrequent and brief, and any improvement in Helen's condition had been imperceptible. What with trying to talk to her, doing the housework, shopping, and attempting to cook meals, Jeremy had no time left to work on Eustace Collinson's book, and even if there had been, he would not have had the energy.

But now, in the second week, with the onset of the school holiday, Rosemary had begun visiting daily, sometimes spending all afternoon with Helen. Jeremy noticed that Helen had begun to be less like an automaton, paying more heed to her surroundings and to what he said to her, sometimes replying in coherent sentences. She'd even begun glancing at the magazines that Rosemary brought her, and in the evenings watching soaps on the television. But she never spoke, nor apparently wished to speak, about her forthcoming trial. Yesterday she'd been visited by a duty solicitor. Rosemary had been present at the meeting. Apparently, Helen had told him she didn't know how she was going to plead. When the solicitor had advised her that she should go for psychiatric assessment so that a report on her mental state could be given to the magistrate, she'd replied that God would be her witness.

All this had been reported to Jeremy by Rosemary. As she'd told him this, Jeremy had noticed that her behaviour towards him had changed. She was polite, but distant to the point of formality, showing no sign of the accord that he thought had been developing between them. What was the matter with her? Had he said something to offend her? Or had Helen said derogatory things about him? *Bloody women.*

But at least now that Rosemary was so often with Helen, he could spend time in his study catching up with re-writing Eustace's manuscript, which was progressing well. But he hadn't had time to work on Stephanie's, even though she'd sent him two new chapters. Today he received an email from her.

Hi, Albert, haven't heard from you for a while. I need your advice. When are you coming up to see me again?

He typed: *I'm afraid I won't be able to make it for some time. I have a few problems at home.*

An instant reply: *Sorry to hear that. Shall we talk? Can you phone me?*

He thought about that. Why not? Rosemary had only just arrived; she and Helen were cocooned together in the lounge, and he wouldn't be disturbed. He emailed back to say he would phone her immediately. He went down to the lounge, picked up the receiver and took it up to his study to ring her.

'Hello, Bertie?'

'Yes. Hello, Stephanie.'

'What's your problem, Bertie? Would you like to tell me about it?'

'It's my wife. She's not well.'

'Sorry to hear that. She's called Helen, isn't she? What's wrong with her, exactly?'

'Well, it's some sort of breakdown. Her mental health isn't too good at the best of times, and something's happened to make it much worse. I can't really leave her until …' he tailed off.

'Until what? Come on, Bertie, we're buddies, aren't we? What are friends for unless we can share problems?'

She's right, thought Jeremy. Now that Rosemary had gone cool on him, he had nobody in whom he could confide. He couldn't go on carrying this burden alone. Though unsure that he wanted the sort of comfort that Stephanie had provided, he desperately needed someone to talk to, and his problem wasn't the sort of thing that he could tell Eustace.

'Stephanie, Helen's in a bit of trouble. She's a teaching assistant at a primary school. A few weeks ago, she lost her temper with a pupil and … well, she hit him. Hello? Stephanie? Are you still there?'

'Sorry, yes, I'm here. That's awful, Bertie. How distressing for you. I quite understand why you can't come up to see me yet. But if you ever feel like talking, be sure to call me.'

'Thank you, I may well do that.'

'I suppose Helen's at home with you? Has she been sacked from her job?'

'No, not sacked. Suspended, pending …'

'Pending what?'

'Oh … an investigation in the school.'

'Well, you look after yourself, Bertie. And I do hope you can come and see me soon.'

'Yes, I'll come up as soon as all this is over.'

'I'll do my best to make you feel better, Bertie. Bye-bye.'

Jeremy felt less isolated after the conversation and began to think about his next meeting with Stephanie. At last, he had something to look forward to. Was it the intimacy which she would no doubt provide that he needed? No, it was just a few hours respite from the hellhole in which he was confined.

***

'Yes!' shouted Stephanie on replacing the receiver. 'It's got to be him!'

She decided to have a celebratory glass of wine. She sat sipping it, congratulating herself on the success of her detective work. Then, she poured herself another glass. She couldn't settle to anything until she phoned Simon, but he wouldn't be leaving his surgery for at least another two hours. And, of course, Jess would be home by the time he got there.

It was a warm sunny afternoon, so she decided to take her third glass of wine into the garden. First, she applied sun cream to her face; she knew a suntan served only to emphasise her wrinkles. How she wished she'd never smoked! She'd given up several years ago, too late, of course, and had tried vaping. But she'd found she was becoming addicted to it even more than she had to cigarettes. It was so easy to suck at a vape constantly, rather like a dummy. So, she'd given that up as well, but oh, how she still longed for a ciggie when a drink was in her hand!

She lowered herself into the deckchair and pulled up her dress. Her legs would look even better with a tan. They were, she knew, her best feature. All her lovers had told her that, as well as saying she had an inviting bum. But now, as she approached 50, the lovers were tailing off. This saddened her. Variety had been the spice of her life.

Sitting on the lawn in her large garden, the far end of which was shaded by sycamore and birch trees, she knew she had much to be thankful for. How fortunate it was that her estranged husband had died before the divorce came through and that she'd inherited the house. It was a pity she had to let out some of the rooms to students, but that was necessary so she wouldn't be forced to look for a job. It gave her the time to dabble in novel-writing, something her husband had always derided, and she'd joined a local writing group, one of whose members she fancied. It had also resulted in her making contact with a copy editor, Albert Rennie, Bertie, though she was now convinced that wasn't his real name.

A breeze was starting to get up, and she felt suddenly chilly. She went inside. Would Simon be home from the surgery? Probably not, but she was impatient to tell him her news. She decided to risk it. If it were Jess who answered the phone, she'd have to think of a reason for calling – invite them for supper tomorrow, maybe?

But her luck and Simon were both in.

'Simon, it's Mum. Is Jess in?'

'No, but she'll be home any minute. Why?'

'I had a phone conversation with Albert Rennie today. He's just got to be who I think he is!'

'Oh, Christ, Mum, you're getting obsessed by all this. You know what I think about it.'

'Look, Simon, we really do need to have a serious conversation about it. Can you come over and see me tomorrow? Doesn't Jess go to her Pilates class on Saturdays?'

'Yes, but – '

'That's settled then. Come over for lunch. Let's go to a pub.'

'Alright.' She registered the sound of resignation in his voice. 'But once we've had the conversation, that's it. Finito. For me, the subject will be closed.'

'Wait until you hear what I have to say before making up your mind. I'll see you tomorrow – about 11.30?'

'Yes, I suppose so.'

'Good.'

She hung up immediately before he changed his mind.

Chapter 21

'So, what time did you say you're meeting your mum?' asked Jessica as she packed her Pilates gear into a holdall.

'About twelve. She wants us to go for a pub lunch.'

'I bet that means she's run out of booze at home.'

Simon laughed. 'Probably. And she likes being in pubs. Always lots of men she can eye up.'

'She never gives up, does she? Why does she want you with her?'

'Oh, she said she just wanted a chat. I thought I'd better oblige. Haven't seen her for several weeks. You know, sweetheart, we really ought to ask her round for a meal soon.'

Jessica, her packing complete, turned to face him. 'Darling, you know I'd be quite happy to invite her round more if only she wouldn't keep on questioning me about my past. You know it upsets me.'

Simon walked over to her, embraced her and kissed her. 'I know, Jess. I'm sorry about that. I'm going to tell her that today. Mmm, you smell nice. You look great in that dress as well.' He ran his hand down her back and caressed her buttocks.

'Don't get me going, Si. You'll make me late for Pilates. Anyway, didn't you get enough last night?'

'I'll never get enough of you, Jess,' he whispered. 'And you're always up for it too, aren't you?'

She kissed him and then disentangled herself from his embrace. 'I suppose you could say that's the one thing that me and your mum have in common. There's one difference though. I only want it from one man.'

'I hope that'll always be the case,' said Simon, watching her as she picked up her hold-all. He still couldn't believe his luck in having her. He'd had to fight off a lot of competition before she'd agreed to come and live with him.

'Okay, I'm off now. See you later, babe. Give my best wishes to your mum. And don't let her get you drunk.'

She blew him a kiss and left.

After completing his medical qualifications, Simon had accepted the offer of a post as junior doctor in his hometown of Leeds. His mother had been delighted, of course, though rather less pleased when he chose to live near his practice in Chapel Allerton rather than closer to her in Headingley.

But he would never regret living and working in Chapel Allerton, for it was there that he'd met Jess. She was working in the local pharmacy, having graduated in chemistry at Leeds University the year before. He'd been attracted to her instantly – who wouldn't have been? He'd got to know her in the course of his duties, began dating her, and found she was not only sexy but intelligent, lively, outgoing and had an engaging sense of humour. She'd had other followers, of course, but to his surprise, he was the only one to whom she granted her favours.

It was not until she came to live with him that he'd found that just occasionally, her zest for life was overtaken by bouts of depression. They didn't last long, and at first, she'd been unwilling to tell him what troubled her. But as their affection for each other deepened into love, she began to open up, and told him a little about her unhappy childhood and adolescence and how she'd fled her home at the age of 16 and, on going to university, had changed her name so her parents couldn't trace her. But she was reticent when he'd asked her how she'd been ill-treated. He'd asked about her father, but beyond saying he wasn't as bad as her mother, she'd been unwilling to talk about either of them. Simon had learned not to press her further – she was happy now, wasn't she?

But one thing he deeply regretted. In the early stages of their co-habitation, he had told his mother what he knew about Helen's past. His mother expressed delight that he'd found a partner, though she never actually said she liked her, and kept quizzing him about her upbringing. He put this down to the fact that she'd started writing a novel and was fascinated by family relationships which apparently formed the basis of much of her writing. She'd never shown him her work, and Simon was grateful for this. He had no interest in literature and would have been unable to make any perceptive observations about it.

Then she'd found that copy editor, Albert Rennie. She talked about him incessantly and began having preposterous theories about who he might be. This had started when she'd read his LinkedIn profile. Simon had thought this was the result of the over-active imagination of an aspiring novelist, but she began to bombard him with what she called evidence. Some of it no doubt resulted from the overnight stay that Rennie had had with her. Simon could well imagine the means she'd probably employed to get the man to talk. He remembered being embarrassed by the way she'd flirted with his university friends whenever they came to visit. They all said his mother was really fanciable, and he suspected that one of them had visited her several times when he'd not been present.

And now, she claimed to have incontrovertible evidence of Rennie's true identity. Whether she had or not, Simon was determined, for Jess's sake, to put a stop to this nonsense for once and for all. He had carefully rehearsed what he was going to say to her when they met for lunch.

When his mother opened the door, he was greeted by, 'You're late! I thought we agreed you'd come at half-past eleven!'

'Well, I had things to do.' In fact, he'd deliberately delayed his arrival; he wanted from the outset to demonstrate he wasn't at her beck and call, as this would set the tone for his responses to whatever it was she wanted to say him.

'Let's get going, then.' She was holding her car keys.

'Which pub are we going to?'

'I thought *The Original Oak*. It's a lovely day, and we can sit in the garden.

'*The Oak*? It's only ten minutes' walk away. You don't need to get the car out.'

'I can't walk there in these heels, can I?'

He looked down. Her stiletto heels were impossibly high. And she was wearing what could only be described as a mini skirt. He wished she wouldn't flaunt her legs. Okay, they were in good shape for a woman approaching 50, but there was no disguising her age when you looked at her face, despite, or perhaps because of, the over-application of make-up. Was she blind to the effect it had on an inelastic wrinkled skin?

'So, if you're driving, does that mean you won't be drinking?'

'Well, if that worries you, you can drive back, can't you?'

First round to her, he thought, then had to smile at his thought, for once in the pub, there'd be no doubting who'd pay for the drinks.

'Come on then, let's go.'

He was surprised to find there were plenty of empty tables in the pub garden before remembering it was the university vacation – no students. His mother sat down and immediately asked for a gin and tonic. He went to the bar. He had already resolved to remain sober so he had his wits about him in the forthcoming conversation, and now that it seemed he'd be driving her home, he had an added reason to ask for just a half of lager. He glanced round at his surroundings as his glass was poured – a large room, modern furniture, but wood panelling on the walls which spoke of earlier times. It was a pub he'd rarely visited as a teenager, and it held no memories for him, but his grandfather often used to speak about the place as it used to be.

He picked up the drinks tray, remembered in time to ask for a menu, and went out to join his mother. She'd put on a pair of sunglasses and was sitting on the bench with her back to the table, her legs on display for all to see.

'Here you are, Mum.' He sat down opposite her, so she had to turn to face him, swinging her legs over the bench as she did so.

'You know, Mum, when I was being served, I started thinking about Grandad and how he used to talk about this place.'

'Really?' She took a swig from her glass. 'Now, Simon, let me tell you what I've found out about -'

'Yes, Grandad always went on about how there used to be a Men Only lounge, even in the 1960s. Woe betide any woman who tried to go in there, apparently. And this garden used to be a bowling green. Did you know that?'

'No, I didn't! And I didn't invite you here to talk about your grandfather!' She took another swig of gin.

Good, she's getting rattled, thought Jeremy. He would have the advantage in the forthcoming conversation if she was flustered and he was coolly dispassionate.

'Listen, Mum, before you start… You don't seem to have understood, despite everything I've said, that I do not want to upset Jess by asking her about her upbringing. We are happy as we are, in the present. Even if the fantasies you have about her past were true, it wouldn't help Jess if I were to tell her. She doesn't need help. She's happy; we're happy.'

He took a first sip of his beer.

'How can you say that when she has those bouts of depression?' she asked.

'And how many times do I have to tell you it's not depression? She just gets down a bit now and again, and not very often.'

'Well, I think it would help her if she came to terms with her past.'

'So you fancy yourself as a psychologist, now, do you? You're talking nonsense, Mum.'

Stephanie emptied her glass. 'Get me another of those, will you?'

'Another one already? What do you want to eat?'

She thrust to one side the menu he gave her. 'I'm not ready to eat yet. Just get me another gin.'

Maybe she needed a few minutes to herself to calm down? She'd begun to talk loudly. As he rose to go to the bar, he noticed that a young couple at an adjacent table were staring at her.

When he returned with her gin, he'd barely had time to sit down before she began talking, her voice lower than it had been.

'Listen, Simon. Just let me remind you of the facts that I've learned about Albert Rennie, and let me finish without interrupting me. One, he lives in Watford, as did Jess. Two, he was a lecturer in an F.E. college, as was Jess's father. Three, his wife's a teaching assistant at the local primary school, as was Jess's mother. Four, his wife has some sort of mental problem. And what I've recently learned is conclusive. His wife has been suspended for assaulting a pupil at the school. There's no doubt in my mind. Albert Rennie has to be Jess's father.'

'What's all this about? Is all this some sort of plot you've devised for your bloody novel? It's all circumstantial. And if by the remotest chance it were true, what would be gained by telling Jess about it? Forget it, Mum. I don't want to hear any more about it, is that clear? Now, have you decided what you want to eat?'

He presumed she was staring at him, but her sunglasses made it uncertain. After a long silence, she spoke.

'I don't feel like eating at all now. After I've finished my drink, you can take me home.'

***

When they arrived back at Stephanie's house, she searched unsuccessfully to find the words to bid Simon goodbye that would not sound dismissive. He was obviously in a similar frame of mind, for he thrust the car keys at her, muttered 'Goodbye', turned round, and marched towards his own car.

She entered the house. She desperately needed to take off her shoes. Her feet were killing her even though she'd spent most of the time seated. She was hot and could do with a shower. On her way to the stairs, she caught sight of herself in the hall mirror. Her lipstick and mascara were smudged, and her blouse had slipped to reveal the wrinkles on her neck. *Oh, Christ, I look like an old whore.* She ran up the stairs, desperate to seek the rejuvenation that cool water might provide.

Back downstairs, refreshed and clad in the one pair of loose jeans she owned, she realised she was hungry, but could be bothered only to cook an omelette. As she busied herself at the stove, she surrendered to the anger that had been welling within her since Simon's departure. It wasn't directed towards him but towards Jess. That bloody girl was coming between her and her son. Stephanie was tempted to invite the two of them round for a meal and to leave on the dining table, accidentally, of course, the photograph of Albert Rennie which she'd had printed.

She sat down at the table and began eating her omelette. She fancied a glass of wine but resisted the temptation; it was only early afternoon, and she'd already had two gins today. Drink always heightened whatever emotion she was in, and she was still nursing angry feelings towards Jessica. She'd settle for a strong coffee after she'd finished her meal.

She took her coffee into the lounge and slumped back in an armchair.

Calm down, woman, she told herself, *think rationally*. The idea of letting Jessica catch sight of the photograph was nonsense; it would only further alienate Simon. She began to wonder why her feelings towards Jessica had changed from indifference to dislike. Then it came to her: catching sight of the raddled ageing woman in the mirror had made her contrast her appearance with that of the pretty, sexy Jessica, a girl who had life in front of her. She was envious to the point of jealousy.

Something else occurred to her; what Simon had said about her actions being prompted by the plot of the novel she was trying to write. Well, in a way they were. It was the interactions between members of families that gave her most inspiration, but she had been finding it difficult to devise a plot with a climactic ending. The idea of Jessica catching sight of a photograph of her father had given her a clue for such an ending. And Bertie was her father, of that she was certain. His real name must be Myers – but no – Myers was the name that Jessica had adopted after she'd left home, wasn't it?

She drained her coffee cup and took it into the kitchen, feeling downhearted. Not only had she alienated Simon, but she now had no idea how to progress her novel. But then, as she put the cup in the dishwasher, the glimmering of an idea came to her. Bertie wouldn't be coming to visit her until the business with his wife was settled, and that could take weeks. That would give her time to restore relations with Simon. She must see him with Jessica more often and never mention Jessica's past. And then – dare she do what had come into her mind?? Yes, she probably would.

She went to phone Simon to apologise for the way she'd behaved and to invite him and Jessica over for the first of what she hoped would be many evening meals before Bertie was able to visit her.

Chapter 22

The day after his conversation with Stephanie, Jeremy was in his study when he received an email from Eustace, asking if he would mind phoning him. Having checked that Helen was with Rosemary in the lounge, he did so. His call was answered immediately.

'Hello, Albert, thanks for ringing. I have a great favour to ask you.'

'What's that then, Eustace?'

'Could you possibly come out to see me at your earliest convenience? I have something I need to tell you, and I'd prefer to do it face to face.'

'Just give me a minute, Eustace. There's something I need to check first.'

He hurried into the lounge. Helen and Rosemary were sitting in adjacent armchairs. They looked up, startled, as he barged in.

'Will you be here tomorrow, Rosemary?'

'Yes, in the afternoon.'

'Good. I've got to go and visit a client, the one in Aylesbury, Helen. I'll only be gone for the day. You don't mind being by yourself before Rosemary comes, will you?'

'No, I suppose not.'

'Good.'

He hurried back into the dining room.

'Hello, Eustace. I can come and see you tomorrow if that's convenient.'

'Yes, the sooner, the better. Will you be here at your usual time?'

While the last sentence was being spoken, Jeremy noticed that Eustace's voice quavered more than usual and was rather hoarse.

'Yes. I will. I'll bring my latest version of your novel with me.'

'There's no need for that. I have something more important to discuss with you. Thanks again for your time. I'll see you tomorrow. Goodbye, Albert.'

Jeremy's delight at the prospect of being released from the house for a day was tempered by Eustace's apparent lack of interest in the novel he was writing for him. He hoped to God that the old boy wasn't having second thoughts about the project.

On this his third train journey to Aylesbury, Jeremy no longer felt the need to check the names of all the stations at which the train stopped. He hardly looked up at all, being immersed in the manuscript in front of him. It was his recently completed chapters of Eustace's story. Although he'd read them through many times before, he wanted to ensure he could remember them accurately, so he need not refer to the typescript when he discussed them with Eustace. He was aware that Eustace had said there were other things he wished to talk about. This still worried Jeremy, and he was determined to keep alive the old boy's interest in the book.

Although Eustace had been happy with what he had written so far, Jeremy himself had reservations about the way he'd approached what was now a novel based on someone's life. He had not been free to adopt the style that he preferred. He had never before written anything from the viewpoint of just one person, and he found first-person narration to be restrictive because he felt a reader needed to get into the heads of other characters in the novel if their motivations were to be fully appreciated.

When he emerged from Aylesbury station, he had to hunch against a gusty wind. The recent sunshine had given way to heavy showers, and more were forecast. He'd had to resort to wearing his shabby raincoat under which were his usual threadbare jacket and baggy trousers. This didn't concern him because Eustace wouldn't notice. The gear that he'd purchased for his visit to Stephanie had been stored in plastic bags at the bottom of his wardrobe, there to wait for his next expedition to Leeds, whenever that might be. He was thankful that he wasn't wearing those trainers. The pavements were awash with puddles.

It had just begun to rain when he reached Eustace's house. He was startled to see a 'For Sale' sign in the front garden. Why on earth would the old boy be moving? He rang the doorbell, and the door was opened by Alisa, Eustace's carer.

'Oh, Mr Rennie,' she said, 'I'm so glad you could make it. Come in.'

Jeremy immediately felt apprehensive. It had been Eustace who'd greeted him on previous occasions.

'Where's Eustace?' he asked.

'Colonel Collinson's in a bad way, I'm afraid. He's gone downhill rapidly in the past few weeks. He's in bed.'

This did not bode well for a discussion about the novel.

'If you don't mind waiting a minute,' said Alisa, 'I'll just nip upstairs to make sure he's not asleep. He dozes off quite often. I think it must be the painkillers. If he is asleep, it won't be for long, so you won't have had a wasted journey.'

Painkillers? Has it come to that? Jeremy remembered Eustace telling him when they first met that he hadn't got long, but there had been no marked deterioration in his condition at their last meeting apart from his being rather more unsteady on his feet.

'He's awake, Mr Rennie, you can go up. Be prepared for him to get tired very quickly.'

What Jeremy wasn't prepared for was the sight of the ashen face on the pillow of the bed in the sparsely furnished room. The eyelids were fluttering, the only sign of life in what could almost be a corpse.

'Albert? Is that you?' The voice was almost a whisper.

Jeremy approached the bed and sat in the chair next to it. 'Yes, Eustace, it's me. I'm so sorry you're ill. What's the problem?'

'Inoperable cancer. I've had it for some time, but not for much longer, I hope. Thank you for coming. I needed to see you before I go to into the nursing home.'

Jeremy struggled to find words. What does one say to someone who reveals he is dying? He muttered an inanity along the lines that he hoped Eustace would be well looked after.

'I'm sure I shall be. Alisa has been wonderful, but it's getting too much for her. And I need constant medication to relieve the pain.'

At least, thought Jeremy, the old fellow was compos mentis. Although his voice was quavery and hoarse, he was still able to articulate sentences. But he doubted that any conversation would involve a discussion about his book.

'Is there anything I can get you, Eustace?'

'No, I can only take liquids. I'm sorry I can't sit up. Can you hear what I'm saying?'

'Yes, perfectly.'

'Good. I have some things to tell you. First, I want to thank you for all the work you've done on my book. It's brought me great pleasure seeing how you're transforming it, and I've enjoyed your visits as well.'

'I've enjoyed writing it, Eustace.'

'I'd like you to finish it, and I'll pay you in advance for that. Then try to get it published under your name. If it sells, you'll get the royalties, of course.'

'Yes, of course, I'll do that. And thank you in advance for the royalties.'

'There's something else. More important.' This statement was gasped rather than spoken.

'Yes? What's that, Eustace?'

There was no reply. His breathing had become laboured, and his head began to move from side to side.

'Are you in pain, Eustace?'

'A bit. Can you call Alisa?'

'Of course.'

Jeremy ran down the stairs and told Alisa she was needed. When she entered the bedroom, he took the opportunity to visit the toilet. His incontinence was getting worse. The pads could hardly cope with the flow. Maybe he should visit the doctor? He reassured himself by thinking how minor his problem was compared to that suffered by Eustace. At least, he hoped it was.

He returned to the bedroom to find Alisa holding Eustace's head up, wiping his mouth. 'There you are, dear,' she said, easing his head back onto the pillow. 'You'll feel better in a few minutes.'

On her way out, she whispered to Jeremy, 'I can only give him oral painkillers. That's why he's going to a nursing home. He needs morphine injections.'

Jeremy sat down beside the bed. 'Take your time, Eustace. Wait till the pain's better before you start talking again.'

He received a nod in return. While he was waiting for him to recover, Jeremy looked round the room. Although it was sparsely furnished, many photographs were hanging from the walls. There was one above the bedhead in which a youthful Eustace in army uniform was standing with a group of soldiers, all grinning, with pints of beer in their hands. Despite his assertions that he hadn't got on with the squaddies, he looked as though he were enjoying himself. Jeremy had never had a crowd of drinking-mates. No such photographs hung on his wall. That had never bothered him before. But now it seemed that Eustace might have had some pleasurable events in his past.

'I'm okay to talk now,' was whispered from the pillow.

Jeremy bent over so his face was close enough to Eustace's.

'The only way I can afford the nursing home fees is to sell the house. I've already had an offer. I think I've only got a few more weeks, hope so, anyway. So, there'll be plenty of money left over from the house sale.' He started breathing heavily again.

'Take your time, Eustace.'

'I've made out my will. You and Alisa will be the only beneficiaries.'

'Eustace, I don't know what to say.'

'Don't say anything. I've got no one else to leave it to. And you've made my final months bearable.'

Jeremy was able only to grasp his hand.

'Listen,' he breathed. 'A word of advice. You're still a young man.'

'I'm 50, Eustace!'

'That's young. Let me tell you something. Old age isn't something that creeps up on you. It starts hitting you, suddenly. It's like walking along a corridor, you hardly notice minor ailments and discomforts, and then suddenly you fall down some stairs. When you get up, you're not the same person. You can't do things you used to be able to. But you try to carry on along the corridor, then you fall down a whole flight of stairs. That's when it really hits you: you're old.'

He started coughing. Jeremy clung onto his hand.

'My advice to you,' he said when the coughing fit was over, 'is to live life to the full while you can. And I suggest you start by getting yourself some decent clothes. That's all. Sorry, want to go to sleep now. Goodbye, Albert.' He closed his eyes.

How does one give a final farewell to a dying man? All Jeremy could say was, 'Goodbye, Eustace. Thank you for your generosity. I'll never forget it. And I'll never forget you.'

Jeremy gave Eustace's hand a final squeeze, got up, and left the room without looking back.

'Has he gone to sleep?' asked Alisa, who was hovering at the bottom of the stairs.

'I think so. Alisa, how long has he got?'

'It's a matter of weeks, I reckon.'

'Where's the nursing home he's going to? Is it local?'

'Yes. It's a good one, privately run. That's why he's selling the house. He didn't want to go into one of those council ones.'

'Will you visit him?'

'Yes, of course.'

'Will you be sure to let me know when … when the end comes? I'll give you my phone number.'

'He's already asked me to do that. He's given me your number. And Mr Rennie – '

'Oh, call me Albert, please.'

'Well, Albert, just in case you were thinking of it, he doesn't want you to visit him there. He doesn't want you to see him in a worse state than he is already.'

'Yes, I understand that. We've said our goodbyes.'

'There's something else he's asked me to do. Come into the sitting room.'

Jeremy followed her in. She went to a battered writing desk, extracted an envelope from the top drawer and handed it to him. It bore his name written in capital letters.

'He asked me to give you this after you'd left him.'

'Do you mind if I open it now?'

'Not at all. I know what's in it.'

Jeremy ripped open the envelope. There was a note inside. It read: *This is payment in advance to you for completing your work on my autobiography, with many thanks for your advice and for your interest and company. You have been a great comfort to me, and I wish we could have met more often. Eustace.* Also in the envelope was a cheque for £1,000.

Jeremy felt a prickling in his eyes, something he hadn't experienced since childhood. He couldn't trust himself to speak and stuffed the envelope into his jacket pocket.

Alisa briefly touched his shoulder. 'It's upsetting, isn't it? He's been very generous to me as well. He's told you about his will, I suppose?'

Jeremy nodded. For the first time, his attention was drawn to Alisa as a sentient being. Previously, he'd barely noticed her; she'd been a mere fetcher-and-carrier, simply doing what she did for the wages she earned. Now she was standing close to him, he noticed that she had beautiful, expressive, large brown eyes.

'I'd better be on my way,' he said. 'I'm sure you've got a lot to do.'

'Just before you do, Albert, I'd like to tell you how grateful I am to you for making my job easier. Before you came on the scene, he was sinking into depression. I was finding that hard to handle, given all the other things I had to do for him. I can never thank you enough.'

Jeremy was unsure who made the first move, but they were embracing.

'Goodbye, Albert.' She kissed him on the cheek.

On the train home, Jeremy was in a daze. A flock of thoughts and emotions fluttered through his brain, none of them alighting for long enough for him to really process them.

The document case which contained his most recent re-write of Eustace's autobiography was on the seat beside him. It had been a waste of time bringing it, for no discussion about it had taken place. In fact, it had been a wasted journey – no! No! How could he think that? Eustace! Poor old Eustace! He would never see him again, would he? The one person in his life with whom he was not only friendly but for whom he felt something like affection.

Then he remembered the envelope in his jacket pocket. He fished it out, opened it, and yes, a cheque for £1,000. That would tide him over for a few weeks, but he needed to get some more clients; otherwise, it would be a case of applying for income support. But wait – what was it Eustace had said – that he should get himself some decent clothes? Why not? Yes, he'd get rid of that ridiculous gear he'd bought for his trip to Leeds, go back to the men's outfitters and get something more suited to a man of his age.

But then his thoughts switched to what Eustace had said about leaving him money in his will. He hadn't really taken it in at the time. How much was it likely to be? How much would a semi-detached house in Aylesbury fetch?

Good God, it could be well over £200,000! Even when Alisa had taken her share, he'd still be a rich man! The prospect staggered him. What would he do with it? The first thing that came to mind was to give up copy-editing and start writing a new novel. Oh, and buy a new computer. And get a mobile phone. And buy some new spectacles. And travel first class on trains. And maybe set himself up as a tutor of creative writing, hire a room for weekly meetings of his students who would pay him a hefty fee?

But the vision that came repeatedly to his mind, interrupting all other thoughts, was that of his farewell to Eustace and Alisa. The mixture of emotions that had welled up within him was like nothing he'd experienced before – pity, sorrow, gratitude, affection. More than affection, it was love, and in Alisa's case, a love devoid of sexual desire. He had managed to put these emotions in the heads of the characters in his novels, but the inspiration for this had largely come from novels written by other people. He finally admitted to himself that he'd often indulged in plagiarism. Well, he wouldn't need to do that anymore. He decided to start writing a new novel immediately.

'Tickets, please!'

He started. The conductor had come up behind him. He pulled his ticket from his wallet and handed it over.

'This is a day return to Aylesbury from Moor Park,' said the conductor.

'Yes, so what?'

'Well, you didn't get off at Moor Park, did you? The next stop's not till Marylebone. I'll have to charge you an excess fare.'

All the charitable thoughts that Jeremy was having for humankind evaporated. He was now faced getting a ticket back to Moor Park when he got to Marylebone, then another ticket for the Metropolitan line train to Watford. He'd be an hour later than the time he'd told Helen he'd be home. Helen! It was the first time he'd given her a thought since leaving her that morning.

PART 4 -AUTUMN

Chapter 23

It was ten o'clock in the morning. Eileen, clutching the local newspaper, had knocked several times on Doreen's door but was still waiting for it to be opened. Usually Doreen visited Eileen, and these visits took place in the afternoon, but Doreen now seemed to be finding it increasingly hard to make herself presentable in the mornings. Eileen was becoming concerned about her friend; her memory, never good, had recently deteriorated rapidly, and she sometimes forgot where things were located in her own house. Eileen had persuaded her to give her a copy of her front door key, so she could enter in case of an emergency.

Just as she was wondering if that day had arrived, the door was opened. Doreen, still in her dressing gown, stood blinking in the doorway.

'Yes?' she said.

'Doreen, it's me, Eileen! Are you alright?'

'Eh? Sorry, couldn't find me glasses.'

That was something that was always happening. But Eileen had noticed that even when Doreen was wearing them, she seemed to find it hard to see. And her hearing wasn't what it was.

'Aren't you going to let me in, dear?'

'Eh? Oh, yes, come in.'

Eileen followed her into the sitting room. The place was a shambles. Eileen thought the time had surely come when her friend needed the help of a carer. She had no family nearby; her daughter had emigrated to Australia years ago, and her son, who lived in Edinburgh, rarely visited her. Eileen had never liked her son. After he'd been to university, he'd become a toffy-nosed individual, and he had an equally snooty wife.

'Sit down, dear. Would you like a cup of tea?'

'Not at the moment, thanks.' Eileen knew that it would take Doreen ages to make it. Staring at her, she was distressed at what she saw. Doreen wasn't looking after herself at all. Obviously, no shampoo had been in contact with her hair for weeks, and there was no getting away from it, her face was dirty, with traces of the remains of breakfast around her mouth and on her chin. Her dressing gown was filthy; God knows what her underclothes were like. Eileen wondered if the time had come to contact Social Services to ask them to pay her a visit. But no, the first thing she'd do when she got back home would be to phone that blasted son of hers and give it to him straight: your mother needs help now, and it's your duty to give it.

But she decided to get on with telling Doreen what she'd come to say.

'Doreen, do you remember telling me you saw Jeremy Johnson running after Helen who was being led away by a man and a woman? That was a few weeks ago.'

'Running after Helen? Yes, I remember. He was shouting at her. Can't remember what he was saying, though.'

'And ever since then we haven't seen anything of Helen, have we?'

'No. Not a sign of her.'

'Well, I've got here our local newspaper. There's a report in it which you'll find interesting.'

Doreen took the newspaper and peered at the page which Eileen had opened.

'Oh, I can't read that small print.'

'Where are your glasses?'

'I don't know. Haven't been able to find them for days. Read it to me, could you, dear?'

'Well, the headline says, *Schoolteacher found guilty of assaulting pupil.*'

'What's that about, then?'

'It's about a hearing at the magistrate's court. The teacher, it was a woman, was given a three-month suspended sentence for assaulting a boy in her class. But the report goes on to say she was a teaching assistant, not a teacher. Can you guess her name?'

'Not Helen Johnson?'

'Right in one.'

Doreen was silent; no doubt, thought Eileen, as dumbstruck as she had been when she first read it.

'There's a lot more here about the trial. Shall I read it all out to you?'

'Ooh, yes!'

Eileen was gratified to see that Doreen's expression was more alert than it had been for weeks. Bad news for the Johnsons, but some people's bad news was good for others. She began reading the article aloud.

***

Yesterday, Rosemary had given Helen and Jeremy a lift home after the court case had ended and had stayed with them until late in the evening going so far as to cook them a meal before leaving. Over the meal, Jeremy had tried to chat about a variety of matters, none of them concerning the trial, and Rosemary had responded in kind. Helen remained silent but calm throughout. After Rosemary had left, Helen went to bed and Jeremy followed soon after. He had fallen asleep almost immediately, emotionally drained after the events of the day.

This morning, preparing breakfast while Helen was still asleep upstairs, Jeremy was trying to come to terms with what was undoubtedly the start of a new phase in his life. He was married to a woman with a criminal record, someone who could never obtain employment as a teacher again. What the hell would she do with her time? Mope around the house, getting in his way, interrupting his writing? And how could he face contact with those who'd doubtless read about the trial and sentence? Could he face going to the *Bricklayers* again and meeting Jim Ellison? His sympathy would be even harder to bear than the undoubted glee of his bloody next-door neighbours. For the first time, he was glad that he had so few contacts in the locality, though no doubt the story would be the talk of the staffroom in the F.E. college, and he imagined members of the Rebel Writers group would rejoice when hearing about his misfortune.

He couldn't face eating anything except cornflakes and a slice of toast and marmalade. As he made himself a cup of tea, he realised he should do his duty as a carer and take one up to Helen. To his surprise, when he entered her bedroom, he found her not only awake but sitting up in bed.

'Tea,' he said. Should he ask her how she was feeling? Might it result in a torrent of tears? He couldn't be doing with that.

She took the cup. 'Thanks.' She sipped at it, then – 'Oh, Jeremy, wasn't Rosemary wonderful in court!'

Well, at least weeping didn't seem to be on her agenda.

'Yes, she was good,' he said. 'Now, if you don't mind, I've got things to get on with.'

'Okay. I'll be getting up soon.'

'No hurry.'

Downstairs and eating his breakfast, he thought about what she'd said about Rosemary. Yes, she was right, Rosemary had been a good character witness, telling the court about Helen's mental state, even hinting that her religious beliefs were partly responsible for her poor self-image, guilt and depression, and that what she was alleged to have done was probably the culmination of years of internal anger. It was probably partly because of her evidence that Helen had been given a suspended sentence rather than being escorted from the dock by a prison officer.

But Rosemary's evidence hadn't been enough for a 'not guilty' verdict to be given. When Jeremy was sitting in the public gallery, he'd been unable to look at Helen when evidence was given by Myrie's father, and statements from children in her class had been read out. According to them, Myrie had banged his head on his desk when falling over after being slapped round the face several times by Helen. When asked how she was pleading, all Helen could say was that she couldn't remember what had happened. It was left to her solicitor to enter a plea of not guilty on the grounds of diminished responsibility. The magistrate, when giving his verdict, said he would be merciful and that a suspended sentence was given on condition that Helen receive psychological counselling to start with immediate effect.

As he washed up the breakfast things, Jeremy hoped that the counselling that Helen was to receive might at least make her less zombie-like so she could use the spare time she'd have on her hands to devote to housework and shopping. He was determined to press ahead with writing a new novel and needed to devote all his time to it. Then, for the first time since the trial, he remembered Eustace's promised bequest. It would be a life-changer. So maybe the new phase of his life would be an improvement on what had gone before?

'Hello.' Helen had entered the kitchen. She was dressed in a sweater and baggy jeans, and he noticed that she'd lost some weight over the past few weeks.

'Do you want some breakfast?'

'Not yet. I'll get it myself later on.'

Her voice was low but calm. She wasn't looking at him but staring round the kitchen. He found it hard to judge her state of mind.

'What are you going to do with yourself today?'

'I'm going to phone Rosemary. I didn't thank her properly yesterday.'

'But the holidays are over. It's Friday, so she'll be at work.'

'Oh. Yes. Well, I'll phone her this evening. I want to tell her how I can repay my debt to her.'

'And how do you propose to do that?'

For the first time, she looked at him. 'I've been thinking about it. Rosemary's a busy woman. I'm going to offer to go round there sometimes and do some housework for her while she's at work. Maybe do some shopping for her. Sometimes, I might stay with her overnight if that's okay by her.'

'And do you think that'll be okay with me?'

'Why shouldn't it be? You can manage by yourself occasionally, can't you? You always say you need time by yourself to get on with your work.'

Jeremy had been wondering for some time when he would tell her about Eustace's bequest. Now he knew he would not be telling her, not yet, anyway.

Chapter 24

Helen had been home for ten days and hadn't yet ventured out alone. She had paid occasional evening visits to Rosemary – Rosemary always collecting her and bringing her back – and on Saturday had spent the day there. Jeremy didn't know if Rosemary had taken up her offer of helping with the housework, but Helen hadn't confirmed this, and Jeremy was not inclined to question her. He didn't want to upset her apparent equilibrium by posing any question that she might regard as being critical.

He had taken her for her first appointment with the psychiatrist, but when he asked how the session had gone, she replied abruptly that she didn't want to talk about it. Otherwise, she was calm, quiet, spoke occasionally about mundane matters such as cooking, washing and ironing, and to tell him which items he should shop for. It was like being with a newly arrived housemate whom he had yet to get to know and who was reluctant to engage in conversation about the inner life she was living. She spent most evenings watching television, and it was a relief when he left her to go and work, or try to work, in his study.

He was in his study this evening, staring at a blank computer screen. The term 'writer's block' was familiar to him but that had never troubled him before, because his two previous novels, still unpublished, had been character-based, and he'd never bothered to plan out a plot in advance because, for him, plots were a secondary concern. He was beginning to realise that the absence of engaging plotlines was the reason for publishers rejecting his manuscripts. No doubt plot-driven novels were much more marketable. So, now he was trying to devise a plot. But nothing came into his head that hadn't been done before by writers of popular fiction. He didn't want to be classed as one of those.

He was relieved when the phone rang downstairs. Helen wouldn't have heard it from the sitting room, so he had an excuse to leave the computer and go down to the dining room to answer it. But it would probably only be Rosemary.

But it wasn't.

'Hello, is that Mr Rennie? Albert?'

'Speaking.'

'Albert, it's Alisa. I'm phoning from Eustace's house. You probably know why.'

'Eustace?'

'Yes. He died last night. I was with him. It was very peaceful.' Her voice was tremulous.

'I'm so sorry, Alisa. But it's probably for the best. And it's good to know you were with him.'

'Yes, I'm glad I was. I held his hand. But I don't think he knew I was there. The painkillers he was on meant he was semi-conscious most of the time. But Albert … before he got to that stage, he used to talk quite a lot, and about you. He kept saying something strange.'

'What was that?'

'He said he hoped when he'd gone and you'd got your inheritance that you'd … well, that you'd be able to come to terms with the 21st century. What did he mean by that if you don't mind me asking?'

'Oh … It was probably all to do with the discussions we had about alienation.'

'Alienation?'

'Alisa, do you know when the funeral will be?'

'Not yet. But I do hope you'll be able to come, Albert. If you can't, I think I'll be the only mourner there.'

'I'll be there, I promise.'

'Oh, good. It'll be nice to see you again.'

'And you too, Alisa.'

'I'll be in touch as soon as I know the date. Bye, Albert.'

'Bye, Alisa, and …'

'Yes? What?'

'Look after yourself.'

Jeremy was neither shocked nor saddened. It was news he had been expecting, and he had come to terms with sorrow during his final meeting with Eustace. It was just another indication that he was entering a new phase in his life, and he was impatient to proceed further, though this would have to wait until he'd received Eustace's bequest.

He'd spent very little of the £1000 that Eustace had given him and remembered that one of the last things that the old boy had said to him was that he should buy some decent clothes. And he'd need formal wear for the funeral, wouldn't he? A proper suit maybe? He could then dispose of the ridiculous gear he'd purchased before going to stay with Stephanie. Stephanie! He had hardly given her a thought for days. There was no prospect of his visiting her yet, not while Helen was so dependent on him. But when, eventually, he could go to see her, he'd wear a suit. That would surprise her, for she knew nothing of his changed financial circumstances. He decided not to tell her. If he were to, she might suggest that he could afford to lower his fees, or even decide to charge him for the services she provided.

The news he'd received might be of interest to Helen. Well, if not of interest, at least something he could tell her which would be something other than the usual brief exchanges about domestic arrangements. He went into the lounge.

He was surprised to find her sitting with a book in her hand. Since the trial, her reading had been confined to magazines. She put the book down when he came in, and he noticed it was *Middlemarch*. Well, if she could concentrate on that epic, she must be feeling better.

'Helen, do you remember I did some copy-editing for a fellow called Colonel Collingwood? I went to visit him in Aylesbury several times.'

'Yes, I remember the name.'

'Well, I've just had some bad news. He died yesterday.'

'Oh.'

'I'll be going to his funeral.'

'When?'

'I don't know yet. I'll be gone for the day. You'll be okay by yourself?'

'Oh, I'll go to Rosemary's. I might stay for two nights.'

Any excuse to go to Rosemary's, he thought as he left the room.

***

Helen threw *Middlemarch* across the room. She couldn't concentrate on it. She'd tried reading it in an attempt to immerse herself in something other than her trial and sentence; magazines had provided little distraction. *Middlemarch* had been a set book in her first year at university, and she remembered having enjoyed it. But she now found it impossible to follow. The storylines were too complex, and there were so many characters that she couldn't keep track of them. *What's happened to me? I've still got my English degree, haven't I?*

At university, she'd envisaged a future teaching English Literature in a secondary school, and by now, would have probably been a senior member of staff teaching Sixth Form students. But her punishment for sinning had been a life constrained by maternal and domestic duties, and having to take a lowly post as a classroom assistant in a primary school.

Now, with her criminal record, she'd never be allowed in a classroom again, not that she ever wanted to be. She knew now that teaching juniors wasn't for her, but what other job could she do? Who would want to employ her? She was condemned to live the rest of her life trapped in the house alongside a man whom she didn't love, didn't even like, and who obviously felt the same way about her. Hadn't she been punished enough?

Oh, forgive me, I'm questioning God's judgement again! This was something she'd begun to do after her trial. She knew why this was; it was because of what Rosemary had said in court when giving evidence as her character witness. She'd said that her religious beliefs were responsible for her mental state and had resulted in her poor self-image and the anger inside her.

Helen hadn't really taken this in at the time, but it must have been lurking sub-consciously in her mind, for in recent days, Rosemary's words had come to haunt her. She even dreamed about them. And she'd begun to think about Jane and the way she'd disciplined her. Might Rosemary be right, that the anger she'd felt about Jane's misbehaviour was the result of her own self-image? And was this anger because of her belief in a judgemental Almighty? Could it possibly be that this belief was mistaken?

The psychiatrist whom she'd visited had tried to get her to talk about her religion. The counselling session hadn't helped her at all. The counsellor hadn't given her advice or comfort. All he wanted to do was to encourage her to talk about herself. She couldn't do it. The counsellor wouldn't have understood.

There was only one person who might understand, and that was Rosemary, who knew all about her upbringing, her beliefs, and how she'd fallen from grace. Yes, she could talk to Rosemary and tell her the thing that was now worrying her above everything else. And an evening's visit to her wouldn't be sufficient. It would take days to try to explain.

Chapter 25

Jeremy and Alisa were standing outside the crematorium waiting for the arrival of the hearse. Alisa had picked him up from Aylesbury station. In just the short drive to the crematorium, a lot had surprised him about her. He'd previously only seen her in her carer's outfit, and he'd hardly recognised the expensively dressed woman who'd stepped out from what looked like an equally expensive car. She'd kissed him on the cheek and complimented him on the suit he was wearing.

'It takes years off you, Albert,' she'd said. He'd remarked that the car wasn't the one which she used to drive to Eustace's, and she'd replied that her son had loaned it to her for the occasion, and she was thinking of buying the same model when Eustace's bequest came through. Throughout their conversation, her voice differed from that which she'd had when a carer. It was louder and laced with short bursts of laughter, and she was using a more sophisticated vocabulary. He'd begun to be aware how little he knew about her.

'Beautiful grounds this crem's set in, aren't they?' said Alisa. 'All these trees! But look, some of them are starting to turn already, mainly the silver birch, oh, and the acers as well.'

'Now you point it out, yes they are,' said Jeremy.

'I don't suppose the beech trees are turning yet. Did you notice on your journey through the Chilterns, Albert?'

'Can't say I did.'

'No, come to think of it, they don't start until October. And it's not till November that they're at their best. It's wonderful walking through the beechwoods then, isn't it? They're almost golden, aren't they?'

'Are they? I never go for country walks.'

'Oh, Albert, you don't know what you're missing! Maybe I can take you on one sometime.'

A car drew up alongside the crematorium entrance, and a bearded elderly man got out and walked towards them.

'Ah, that's the officiant,' said Alisa. 'Nice chap. I 've told him all about Eustace so he knows what to say.'

'Mrs Gooder, hello again.' Jeremy realised that he hadn't known Alisa's surname, nor that she was married, though, of course, there was no reason why she shouldn't be.

'Mr Molyneux, can I introduce Mr Rennie.'

Hands were shaken. 'Do I take it,' said Molyneux, 'that you two are the only mourners?'

'Yes. I thought we might be.'

'Very sad. Well, I'll do my best to give Colonel Collinson a dignified send off. Oh, here comes the hearse.'

The vehicle drew up, four pallbearers dismounted and pulled the coffin, devoid of any wreaths, out onto a trolley. Molyneux took up position at one end of it, and with a nod to the pallbearers, led the way into the crematorium, Jeremy and Alisa following behind.

Jeremy was overwhelmed by the vastness of the room they entered. It had a high ceiling, bare walls, large windows, and row-upon-row of benches, enough seating to accommodate fifty people. The almost-empty room epitomised Eustace's solitary existence. Jeremy could not help but wonder – who would attend his own funeral? Helen, he supposed, Rosemary maybe, perhaps Jim Ellison? What about Stephanie? Probably not. Alisa? Maybe, if she got to know him better. Only four people! And which of them, if any, would be able, or even willing, to brief an officiant so his life could be eulogised? None of them had read, or even knew about, the books he had written. None of his former students, even if any remembered him, would have praised his teaching. He was swamped by a profound sense of isolation, more than that, a sense of worthlessness.

They took the bench at the front, facing the podium onto which the coffin was manoeuvred by the pallbearers. Molyneux stepped forward.

'Welcome,' he said. 'I cannot claim to have known Colonel Eustace Collingwood. What I have to say has largely been written by Mrs Alisa Gooder, who was his carer for many years.' He cleared his throat, referred to his notes, and began reading.

Listening to the reading, Jeremy was taken aback by how much Alisa knew about Eustace's life. He had obviously confided in her. There was even a reference to how he had some regrets about his time spent in the army, though no specific mention was made of his actions in Northern Ireland. As the reading went on, it was evident that Alisa had become very fond of him, how despite his long illness, he'd always been kind and considerate to her, and how she felt able to confide in him about her own life. And Jeremy was struck by the articulate prose in which the eulogy had been written. Had Ailsa really written all that? Or had she just provided notes on which Molyneux was basing his address?

Molyneux concluded by saying that Eustace's favourite piece of music would be played, during which the mourners could think of him and, if any had religious beliefs, to offer a prayer for him. The music began playing. It was a choir singing 'I Vow to Thee My Country', something that Jeremy remembered from his schooldays. He felt his throat constricting, and he heard Alisa quietly sobbing. He reached for her hand, and she clung onto it.

When the music stopped, the officiant stood in front of the coffin, bowed, and walked towards the door, a signal to Jeremy and Alisa that they should do the same. As they walked out, Jeremy was thankful that he'd not had to witness the coffin descending into the abyss accompanied by the creaking of pulleys, as had happened at his father's funeral.

'Thank God that's over,' said Alisa after they had bid goodbye to Molyneux. 'I don't know about you, Albert, but I could do with a stiff drink. Would you like to come back to my place before I take you back to Aylesbury?'

'Yes, I'd like that very much, Alisa.'

Chapter 26

'Here you are, Albert, I think you'll find this touches the spot.'

Jeremy took the glass of whisky from her and took a sip. He was getting to like the stuff. He'd better be careful; it would be all too easy to indulge when he became a rich man.

Alicia sat down in the armchair opposite him, holding what looked like a gin and tonic.

'Albert, I haven't told you that I'm the executor for Eustace's estate, have I? I don't think it'll be long before it's all settled. Of course, I'll let you know when it is. D'you know how you're going to spend your inheritance?'

'I haven't really decided yet. I've spent a lifetime having to count the pennies. It's like stumbling on a treasure trove and not knowing what to do with it. How about you?'

'Well, I'm quite comfortably off, as you've probably noticed.' She gestured around the tastefully furnished lounge. Jeremy assumed the rest of the house, a largish detached, was similarly equipped. 'I have my late husband to thank for that, bless him. He was a solicitor.'

'How long have you been widowed, Alisa?'

'Ten years. Cancer. At least he lived long enough to see our son graduate. This house is a bit too big for me, but I've never wanted to move. All my friends are round here. I think I'll give my son some of my money; he's still young enough to enjoy it.'

'How long have you worked as a carer, Alisa?'

'Years. I started out as a hospital nurse, but I got fed up with some of the doctors. They were so arrogant, so I moved to working in a care home. It was okay, but there were so many residents, lots with dementia, and it was impossible to spend time chatting to them and getting to know them. So I started working for a company that provides care in people's houses. I enjoy it. I won't be giving up the job even with the money I'm coming into.'

Jeremy was struck by how content she seemed with her lot, yet there was no trace of smugness. While she was talking, he observed her closely for the first time. Even with her smart attire, her discreetly applied make-up, and her blonde hair, she was not what one could call attractive, apart from her large brown eyes. She was overweight with stumpy legs half- disguised by a skirt that came down to mid-calf.

'Albert! Did you hear me?'

'Eh? Oh, sorry. I was just thinking about what you told me. What were you saying?'

'I said that was enough about me. What about you? I don't know anything about you apart from what Eustace told me. Do you have lots of clients like Eustace was? Are you married? Do you have children?'

Jeremy, hesitantly at first, then, with occasional promptings from Alisa, found himself telling her first about his career, then about his personal life. He found himself explaining why he'd had to marry, and then told her about Jane.

'It doesn't sound like a very happy marriage, Albert – oh! I'm sorry! that was most insensitive of me. It's none of my business.'

'No, I'll tell you about it.'

He began to elaborate. It was the first time he'd ever opened up to anyone, the first time he'd ever encountered anyone who would probably listen sympathetically. As he continued to speak, he became increasingly emotional. What was happening to him?

'I've never spoken to anyone about this before, Alisa. I think it was Eustace's funeral that's made me feel this way. In the crematorium, I realised how few people would mourn my death. I felt isolated and worthless and ....'

He stopped in mid-sentence, aware that his voice was beginning to quaver. Alisa rose from her chair, came over and sat on the arm of his. She put her arm round his shoulder and kissed his cheek. He began to cry. Alisa kept her arm round him. The last time a woman had given him this sort of affection was when as a child his mother had embraced him and comforted him after he'd been bullied at school. He still missed his mother, even though nearly forty years had passed since her death.

Eventually, he stopped crying. Alisa kissed him again, then returned to her chair.

'Albert, would I be right in thinking all that was something you've never spoken about before?'

'Yes. You're right.'

'Well, I hope you feel better for it.'

'Yes, I do. And there's something else I need to tell you. My name's not Albert Rennie.'

Alisa's eyes widened. 'I don't understand.'

'It's a name I adopted for my business. Albert Rennie Literary Agency. My real name's Jeremy, Jeremy Johnson.'

'Oh, I see. Well, at least I think I do. I'll have to get used to calling you Jeremy. It won't be too difficult; you don't look like an Albert.'

'It's strange, Alisa, but over the past few weeks, I've begun to admit to myself that I've been hiding under the name Albert Rennie.'

'What do you mean?'

'It's the name of the persona I adopted. In fact, I adopted that persona long before I gave him a name. It started when I was at school, when I knew I'd never fit in with – '

'Woah, Alb … Jeremy! I don't want this to be a confessional. I want to get to know you as you are. If you'd like that, well, you could always come over and see me again, couldn't you?'

'I'd like that very much.'

'What time did you say your train was?'

'Half-past three.'

'Right. Let me rustle up something to eat before I get you to the station.'

Chapter 27

Helen wasn't in the sitting room when Jeremy arrived home. Perhaps she was in the kitchen? She wasn't. Nor was she in the dining room. Surely, she hadn't gone to bed already? It was only six o'clock. *Oh God, has she had a relapse?* He hurried upstairs, knocked on her bedroom door. No response. Asleep already, maybe? He entered. She wasn't there.

Where the hell could she be? He went back down to the kitchen, and there he noticed on the table a scrawled note. *Gone to Rosemary's for the weekend. She'll bring me back on her way to work on Monday morning.* It wasn't signed.

Should he phone to ask if she was alright? *No, why the hell should I?* If she wasn't well, Rosemary could look after her. His initial anger at the abruptness of her note subsided when he realised that, in fact, he was relieved. He could do with a weekend alone to ponder over the events of the day, a day which had begun with sadness which had then turned into desperation but had ended with something approaching contentment. He would be seeing Alisa again, of that he was certain.

The stock of ready meals in the refrigerator was running low, but a pizza would suffice for this evening. As he waited for it to heat up, he began thinking about Stephanie. Soon he wouldn't need the income from copy-editing her novel, and he was now certain that he no longer required the service she provided for him. Should he end all contact with her?

But how should he terminate the relationship, if such it could be called? A letter or email would appear insultingly aloof, given the intimacy which they'd shared. A phone call, maybe? But a telephone explanation might be misinterpreted because facial expressions and body language couldn't be used to soften the message he wanted to give, and in any case, he knew he would be frequently interrupted. There was no alternative. He would have to see her one more time and explain his decision to her as politely as possible, though he had no clear idea of what he could say about the reason for it. He made up his mind. He would phone her after his dinner to arrange a date to visit her.

'Hello? Stephanie? It's Albert.'

'Bertie! How good to hear from you. How are things?'

'Oh, not so bad.'

'How are things with that wife of yours? Has she been suspended from school? Does that mean you're lumbered with her?'

'She's been sacked.'

'I should think so too. Hitting a schoolkid! Has she done that sort of thing before?'

'Look, Stephanie, Helen sometimes goes to stay with a friend. In fact, she's with her now, and – '

'You mean she's actually got a friend?'

''She's started to stay with her friend at weekends. So, would a weekend visit to you be okay?'

'Yes, of course, Bertie! And you can stay as long as you want. When can you come?'

'Next weekend, I think. I'll confirm that as soon as I can.'

'It'll be so good to see you, Bertie! And more than just see you, I hope.'

'Yes. Well … look, I've got to go now, Stephanie. I'll phone again on Monday when I'll be sure I can come.'

'Looking forward to it already, fuckbuddy. Bye, Bertie.'

'Goodbye, Stephanie.'

***

'Yes!' Stephanie shouted after she'd replaced the receiver. Things were working out as she'd hoped. After several visits from Simon and Jessica for evening meals, relations with them had improved. She never mentioned Jessica's past, and took pains to compliment her on her appearance.

Simon seemed to have forgiven her for her behaviour at the pub.

The time was now right. But she'd have to wait for Jeremy to confirm his visit before she could contact Simon to issue a further invitation to dinner. It was like writing the final chapters of a novel and still not knowing how the story would end. Which was exactly how she wanted it to be.

Chapter 28

Rosemary was still unsure if it was wise to have Helen to stay for the weekend. She thought it best to keep her visit secret. She had waited until dusk had fallen before collecting her, and on arrival, had parked in the driveway with the car interior lights turned off until she'd been sure that nobody was around to see Helen enter the house. The time spent in the car had been made uncomfortable as a result of Helen's body odour.

Once inside, Rosemary decided to be frank with her before taking her into the lounge.

'Helen, you do realise you're taking a risk leaving your house without telling the authorities where you'd be going? And I'm taking a risk as well. If anyone from the school were to see you with me and reported it, I could be for the high jump.'

'Yes, I know.''

'So, you mustn't leave the house, not even go into the garden, and I'd prefer it if you didn't look out of the front windows.'

'Yes.'

'I've put you in the back bedroom. Make sure you pull the curtains before you turn the light on; otherwise, the neighbours might see you.'

'Yes, I will.'

'Good. Now, if you'd like to go through to the lounge, I'll take your things up to your bedroom. Oh, have you eaten this evening?'

'Yes'.

'D'you fancy a cup of tea? And I've got some cake to go with it.'

'Just tea.'

As she made the tea, Rosemary was wondering what she'd let herself in for. She'd witnessed Helen in a variety of moods – depressed, silent, tearful, self-denigrating, and on rare occasions at school, even aggressive – but this evening there was something different about her. Her responses to the remarks Rosemary had made had been almost monosyllabic and delivered in something akin to grunts. Throughout their short conversation, she'd not made eye contact: her head jerked, not only from side to side, but up and down. After she'd given Rosemary her overnight bag, her hands flew across her breast, almost as though she were warding off an attack. If the change in her behaviour was a result of her counselling session with the psychiatrist, then this did not bode well for future sessions.

Rosemary carried the tea into the lounge to find Helen standing erect in the middle of the room, gazing around as though she'd never been there before. Seeing her standing, it was apparent that she'd lost a lot of weight in the space of just a fortnight. The phrase 'her clothes hung on her' was entirely apt: her shoulders were now so bony it was as though her cardigan were dangling from a coat-hanger.

'Do sit down, Helen.'

She obeyed. Rosemary placed her teacup on the table in front of her, then sat down in the chair opposite. Helen made no move to pick up the cup but continued to stare round the room.

'Well now, dear. I assume Jeremy knows you're staying – '

'Are you still a sinner?' The interruption was not shouted but grunted.

'I beg your pardon?'

'Your gentleman friend. Does he still come to visit you?'

Rosemary had completely forgotten the excuse she'd given when Helen had previously asked to stay with her.

'Oh, I think you must have misunderstood me, Helen. My friend and I have a platonic relationship.'

There was no indication that Helen had heard her. She said nothing. Her teacup remained untouched. But she turned her head and looked Rosemary in the eye.

'Do you believe in the Almighty?'

Rosemary took a sip of tea, wondering what sort of reply Helen would find least offensive. But at least she'd started speaking in sentences.

'Helen, I think I've told you before that I'm agnostic.'

'So, you think the Almighty might exist?'

'Possibly. But there's no way of proving it one way or the other, is there? Listen, Helen. I went to a Church of England primary school; it was the only school in my village. But the God I was taught about was very different to the one which you seem to believe in. Your tea's getting cold.'

Helen glanced at her cup but made no move to pick it up. She was gazing fixedly at Rosemary.

'What do you mean?'

'Well, from what I remember, we were told at school that God would forgive any wrongdoing if we prayed for forgiveness.'

'Even if you committed a mortal sin?'

'I'm sorry, Helen, but I don't really know what a mortal sin is. It was something never mentioned in my R.I. lessons. And by the time I got to hear the term, I was no longer a Christian.'

'Well, I committed one, didn't I?'

'So you say. But why are you so sure that you haven't been forgiven?'

There was no reply. Helen's gaze left Rosemary's face and darted round the room. Then she put her hands on her temples and let out a howl of anguish.

'I don't know! I'm not sure of anything anymore!' She began weeping.

Rosemary went across and touched her shoulder. It was the closest contact she'd had with her since being in the car and her need to use a deodorant was again apparent.

'Helen, let's not talk about this tonight, you'll only get more upset. Try and drink your tea, and then I suggest you have an early night. We can carry on talking tomorrow if you feel up to it.'

Helen reached for her cup and lifted it shakily. Once she'd taken a sip, Rosemary left her and went up to her bedroom to collect her sleeping pills. They'd worked last time Helen had taken them. Rosemary thought she'd take one as well. She'd need a good night's sleep if she were to be able to cope with what was threatening to be a demanding weekend.

The sleeping pill certainly worked. It was 8.30 when Rosemary woke from a dreamless sleep. She instantly remembered that she had a guest. She heaved herself from the bed and struggled into her dressing gown, at the same time girding her loins to prepare for whatever scenario awaited her today. Then she heard, coming from downstairs, what sounded like the clattering of crockery. *Oh God, what's she doing down there?*

She hurried downstairs. The kitchen door was open. She was confronted by Helen, fully dressed, standing in front of the table on which were cups, plates and a carton of milk.

'Oh, you're up already, Helen. How did you sleep?'

'I've found the milk in the fridge. Where do you keep your teabags and sugar? And cornflakes, do you have them for breakfast? And what about toast? I don't see where you keep bread.' Her voice was no longer a series of grunts, and her tone was rather like the one she had when she'd first taken responsibility for a class, assertive and verging on the demanding.

'Helen, you're my guest. There's no need for you to do this.'

'Yes, there is! I have to do it! I need to be useful!'

Rosemary was about to tell her to calm down but thought better of it. 'Well, it's very nice of you to help, dear. I don't use teabags, but the tea's in the cupboard over there and so's the sugar. I'll get out the cornflakes and bread.'

Between them, they organised the items on the kitchen table, Rosemary sometimes having to adjust their positions from where Helen had clumsily placed them. Breakfast was eaten in near silence. Rosemary couldn't think of an opening conversational gambit, and Helen was devouring her meal as though she hadn't eaten for weeks.

'I'll do the washing up,' said Helen after she'd finished eating.

'Oh, there's no need to do that, just put things in the dishwasher.'

'Don't know how to use it. I've never had a dishwasher.'

'Well, all right, if you don't mind washing up, I'll go and get dressed while you're doing it.'

As she put on her clothes, Rosemary was trying to work out what might transpire from Helen's change of mood. But whatever her state of mind, how on earth would they spend the day? What could they talk about, trapped inside the house together? It would do Helen good to have a change of scene, to be taken out in the car, see the countryside, maybe visit a café in a village somewhere. But that would be risky. A neighbour might see her when she walked from the front door to the car.

She'd just got to the top of the stairs when she heard the sound of something breaking. She entered the kitchen and found Helen bent over by the sink.

'What's happened, Helen?'

Helen rose to face her. She was clutching the shards of a teacup, one that had been used at breakfast, one of the set that had been given to Rosemary as a wedding present by her grandparents.

'Oh, Helen, not one of my cups! How did you manage to drop that?'

'The water was too hot! It burnt my hand, so I pulled it out and dropped the cup I was washing. I couldn't help it, could I?' As she spoke, her voice became shriller.

'Why didn't you use the rubber gloves? Look, they're on the draining board.'

'Because I didn't see them! You didn't tell me they were there! How was I supposed to know?' She was now screaming. 'I suppose it's my fault, isn't it? Everything's my fault!'

'Helen, please – '

'I'll show you what's my fault!' She grabbed a plate from the table and hurled it across the room. It smashed against the refrigerator. 'See, that's my fault! And so's this!' She picked up a cereal bowl, looked round the room as though searching for something to aim at, then threw it at Rosemary. It missed her, just.

Rosemary advanced towards her, arms outstretched, determined to prevent any more damage and to ward off the possibility that she might be assaulted. Leroy Myrie's fate had come to mind. But Helen made no further move. She just stood staring into space. Then her posture underwent a total change, her shoulders slumped, her head bent towards her chest, she seemed almost to be shrinking.

'Oh, Rosemary,' she moaned. 'I'm sorry. Please help me. Only you can help me.'

'Of course I will, dear.' Rosemary put her arm round her shoulders, thinking as she did so that visits to the psychiatrist seemed to have resulted in Helen's worsened state. 'Come on, let's get you into the lounge.' She led her there and settled her in an armchair.

'Rosemary … I hate myself. But it's worse than that. I've … I'm …'

'Take your time, dear.'

'I'm not sure I believe in God anymore. But how can I live without my faith?'

At least, thought Rosemary, she was calmer. But she seemed to be inviting advice on her religious beliefs, and this was something that Rosemary felt totally unqualified to give, even if the discussion were to be rational, and that was something she doubted.

'Helen, you obviously have things you'd like to tell me. I think it would do you good to talk, and I'm happy to listen for as long as you want me to. But I think you need to relax before you start. Would a bath help? I always find lying in hot water beneficial whenever I've had a trying day.'

'Yes, that would be nice.'

'Good. I'll go and run the bath and sort out a towel for you. Help yourself to anything else you might need, like moisturiser, oh, and deodorant.'

Chapter 29

Helen had spent nearly an hour in the bath, constantly topping it up with hot water, something that wasn't possible to do at home because their antiquated immersion heater never behaved itself. Rosemary was right: she felt better than she had for days. She climbed out and patted herself dry. There was no need to hurriedly scrub herself as she did at home because Rosemary's bathroom was wonderfully warm, being equipped not only with a radiator but a fan heater. Moisturiser, talcum powder and spray-on deodorant were laid out on the granite surface next to the washbasin, and she made full use of them, something she was no longer in the habit of doing. If only she'd brought some clean underclothes with her. She sniffed her blouse before putting it on and it reeked of sweat – what must Rosemary think of her? She'd have to keep her cardigan on in the hope it would serve as a barrier.

Although she felt calmer, she was unsure what she could say to Rosemary to atone for the way she'd behaved. Occasionally, after her outbursts of rage or hours of depressed anguish, she recognised these as being symptoms of mental illness. But this recognition failed to prevent their recurrence, and it had been almost a comfort to believe that God taught sinners by causing them to suffer, and that by suffering she might one day be absolved of her sins. But now she was uncertain about this. It was impossible to talk to Jeremy about it. Rosemary would at least listen sympathetically.

Rosemary was in the lounge, sitting reading a newspaper.

'Ah, Helen! You've had a long soak, haven't you? Do you feel better for it?'

'Yes, much better. Rosemary, I'm so sorry for the way I behaved. I don't know what – '

'Let's hear no more of it, dear. Can I get you anything? Tea, coffee?'

'Not at the moment, thanks. I want to try and explain things.'

'Sit down, then. And take your time. We've got all day. And promise me one thing – you won't keep apologising.'

Helen sat down and was silent for several minutes. She didn't know how to start. She told Rosemary so.

'Well, I've often thought that I know nothing about your childhood or your upbringing. Why don't you start by telling me about that? What sort of school did you attend?'

'I didn't go to school.'

'What?'

Helen began to talk about her childhood. She found it easier to recount things about her distant past than to try to explain her current religious uncertainties. So she explained that her parents had provided home tuition until her early teens, but then they'd hired visiting tutors to assist with coaching her for her GCEs and then for her A Levels. She assumed that the tutors had been vetted to ensure that they were believers. This meant she had little contact with people of her own age; her social life was limited to accompanying her parents on visits to those of a similar faith to theirs. Once she began studying for A Levels, she was allowed to spend time in the local library on the understanding that she was to go straight there and come straight home and under no circumstances to visit coffee bars.

'But Helen,' Rosemary interrupted, 'surely by the time you reached about 16 you must have felt imprisoned? Didn't you want to meet other teenagers? Weren't you tempted to rebel?'

'No. I didn't have any idea what life was like for young people devoid of faith. We didn't have a television or radio, and my parents didn't take a newspaper.'

'But what about the books you studied for A Levels? You did English Literature, didn't you? Didn't modern novels give you some idea about how life was lived by people outside your faith? About how people misbehaved, about crime, and dare I say it, sex? The sort of things that fascinate most teenagers?'

Helen explained that her tutors had told her that some of the set texts were works of the devil, written to lead people into temptation, but that she should nevertheless try to suspend her revulsion for the sake of achieving success in her examinations. But she couldn't bring herself to admit to Rosemary that even by the time she reached 18, she had no clear idea about precisely what sexual relations involved. Not having attended school, she had received no sex education. It was something her parents never spoke of.

'What I don't understand, Helen, is why your parents allowed you to go to university, given that they wanted to restrict your contact with other young people.'

'They wanted me to get a degree so I could teach and pass on the word of God to children. And they arranged for me to live in digs where the landlady was one of our faith.'

'But surely you must have got to know your fellow students? The ones on your course?'

Helen struggled to articulate her response to that, for it was interaction with her peers that eventually led to growing feelings of guilt. She told Rosemary that she was successful in avoiding contact with those men and women who made it all too obvious that they relished the opportunities that came their way to behave immorally. She'd sought out the company of the demure, the serious, the unfashionable. But then even some of *them* began to crack dubious jokes and make references to sex. As time went on, she began to experience strange sensations in her body. It was this that resulted in her feelings of guilt. However much she'd prayed to be free of these sensations, they hadn't disappeared; indeed, they'd grown stronger.

Rosemary listened to all this without commenting. Helen stopped talking. She was exhausted from the effort of revealing things that she'd previously hardly dared admit to herself.

'Do you want to stop now, Helen? You've already told me what happened at the party after finals, how Jeremy took advantage of you. Shall we have a coffee? Then you can go on to tell me about your religious doubts. Or we can leave that till later if you want.'

'No, I don't want coffee, Rosemary. I need to tell you exactly what happened at that party.'

'Okay, dear. Carry on.'

'I got to like Jeremy more than anyone else of the course. He never made crude jokes. He listened when I talked about my faith. He wasn't like a young man. He didn't dress like one, and he was a man out of his time, somehow. We began spending time together. We never went out in the evening, but we used to go to the university coffee bars together. We talked about the books we were studying.'

'Did he … well, did he seem to be getting fond of you?'

'I think he just saw me as a friend.'

'And was that how you saw him?'

'Yes, but … but I began to have those strange sensations in my body when I was with him. And sometimes when I just thought about him. I came to understand what they were because I'd overheard some of the tarty women on the course talking about how they felt sometimes in the company of men. They had no shame.'

Rosemary made no comment about this, but Helen noticed a slight lifting of her eyebrows.

'Anyway, after finals were over, one of the students organised a party to celebrate. It never occurred to me to go, but Jeremy said we ought to because some of his serious friends were going, and it might be the last time we'd all be together, apart from at the degree ceremony, of course. So, we went. It was held in a flat shared by three of the tarty women.'

'That must have been a revelation for you.'

'It was like walking into hell. The room was dark. There was deafening music, people shouting, dancing, or kissing and cuddling. Everybody was drinking. I sat down with Jeremy at the side of the room, but one of the women came up and grabbed Jeremy and told him she was going to dance with him. She pulled him to his feet, and he began shuffling about with her. I was left alone. But then one of the quieter men came up to me and asked if I wanted a drink. I didn't want to be left alone, so I said yes, an orange juice. Oh, my Lord, Rosemary, I'm finding this so difficult to talk about.'

'You don't have to, dear. Let me guess. Did the man lace your drink with alcohol?'

'He must have done because it tasted a bit strange. But it gave me a warm feeling inside. He got me another one and sat down next to me and started talking. Then I noticed that Jeremy wasn't dancing anymore, but he was standing talking to the woman. He was drinking as well. By this time, the music had stopped, and a lot of people seemed to have left the room. I caught Jeremy's eye, and he came straight over. The man sitting next to me got up and left. Jeremy sat down and took my hand, and said he was sorry he'd left me. Then he put his arm round me. Oh, Rosemary, it was so comforting. So I … I kissed him. He began cuddling me, giving me long kisses, and I began to get those feelings inside me.'

'So it wasn't Jeremy who got you drunk?'

'No. But I think he was drunk as well. Everything became a blur. I can vaguely remember us leaving the room and going upstairs to a bedroom. Jeremy told me afterwards that it was the woman who he'd been drinking with had told him her bedroom was available. When we laid down on the bed, I knew …I knew I wanted him.'

'And was the night Jane was conceived?'

'Yes. You must see now that the sin was mine.'

'Helen, you look exhausted. You sit there. I'll go and make us some coffee.'

*****

Rosemary was reeling from listening to Helen's confession – yes, there was no other word for it. Not that she had anything to be ashamed of. So, she'd had sexual feelings? Who hadn't? But she was still referring to Jane's conception as a sin. She'd hinted that she now had doubts about her faith but had thus far said little about that.

Rosemary wasn't sure she had the energy to cope with a further torrent of remorse from Helen. Why had she taken on the responsibility for helping her? She wasn't qualified to adopt the role of a mental health counsellor, not that the one Helen was seeing seemed to be doing her much good. Rosemary felt she had become trapped in this role as a consequence of being Helen's mentor at school. And there was a sense of guilt that stemmed from her not intervening earlier when Helen had first exhibited signs of instability in the classroom.

As she made the coffee, an idea came to her. Yes, she *would* take her out for a ride in the car, and if the neighbours saw her, well, she'd face that problem later. She had to get her out of the house, show her some pleasant countryside, maybe call into a pub somewhere for lunch. She would insist that Helen didn't mention her religious beliefs until they returned this evening. And, given that she was staying the night, there was always tomorrow.

Chapter 30

'We'd better be off, Jess,' said Simon.

'Yes, I'm more or less ready. I'm not going to bother tarting myself up. Your mum goes over the top paying me compliments all the time. It's beginning to piss me off a bit.'

'Oh, c'mon, Jess. She's just trying to be nice. You must admit she's easier company than she used to be. And she never mentions your past now, does she? I think I really got through to her that time I met her in the pub.'

'Yeah, it looks like it. But why is she insisting we stay the night? We haven't done that for ages. I don't like that bedroom. It's miles down the corridor to the bathroom. Why's she got the en-suite in that small room with the single bed?'

'Search me. Perhaps that room's reserved for her gentlemen friends.'

'Huh. If that was the case, it'd have a double bed in it.'

'Jess, darling, I just hope you'll be as rampant as she is when you reach her age.'

'You needn't worry about that, Si.' She put her arms round him and kissed him. 'Just so long as you can still get it up.'

'You never know, I might have to resort to little blue pills. Come on, it's time we were off.'

***

'Bertie! How lovely to see you!' Stephanie embraced him. 'Come in. Hey, that's a very smart suit you're wearing. Takes years off you. And you look much better now you've let your hair grow longer. Fancy a coffee, or a cup of tea? Or something stronger?'

'A bit early for me, Stephanie. Coffee will be fine. I'll just take my case up to my room.'

'You ought to leave your washing and shaving gear here, now you can come more often. All you need bring with you is a clean shirt. Oh, and a pair of clean underpants, of course.'

'I'll be back down in a few minutes, Stephanie.'

As he put on a fresh incontinence pad, Jeremy was wondering how soon he should tell her that this would be his last visit and that this one would not involve the sort of activity that she was obviously expecting. Should he tell her immediately, perhaps, and then find himself ejected from the house before he could even call a taxi? If only he'd bought a mobile phone with Eustace's £1000. He was still debating how and when he should approach the matter as he went downstairs and joined her in the lounge.

She was sitting on the settee, her skirt pulled up to mid-thigh. She patted the seat next to her, and he decided it would be politic to comply. If he told her what he'd come to say, he'd probably be banished immediately, and he could do with a coffee after his journey. Then he noticed there were no cups on the table in front of her.

'I'll get you your coffee in a minute, Bertie. Let's have a bit of a cuddle first.' With that she pulled him towards her and kissed him, her tongue teasing the inside of his mouth. 'I've missed that, Bertie,' she said when she released him.

'Have you?'

'Oh, well, yes. But don't you want to talk about your writing first?'

'We've plenty of time for that. Anyway, I've got something to tell you which might surprise you.'

Jeremy was immediately apprehensive. Hadn't she sprung enough surprises on him during his first visit?

'What's that then?'

'We'll be having company this evening. I've invited my son and his partner to join us for dinner.'

'Oh. Um … well, I'll be pleased to meet them.'

'The reason I've asked them is because the new novel I'm writing will be based partly on his partner's life. She doesn't know that yet. She's called Jessica, by the way. I thought that because you're so interested in character portrayal in novels, you might like to see what she's like.'

'Well, yes, but if it's a novel, a character should be the product of the author's imagination, and – '

'And they'll be staying the night. Simon won't want to drive back after he's been drinking.'

'Staying the night? Really?'

'Oh, don't worry, Bertie! Their bedroom is at the far end of the corridor from yours. I'll give them some time to settle down before I come and join you.'

***

Stephanie hadn't prepared an evening meal. She had ready-meals in the fridge just in case Simon stormed out taking Jessica with him as soon as he realised what was afoot. But not, she hoped, before she could witness the reactions of Bertie and Jessica when each came to realise whom the other was, and what they then said to each other.

But Bertie didn't seem relaxed. She'd assumed that after their last encounter he'd be more affectionate, more tactile. He hadn't responded in the way she'd anticipated when she'd kissed him. It was as though he had something else on his mind.

But *she* wasn't entirely relaxed either because Simon and Jessica were late. She still was unsure how to effect the introductions – should she introduce Bertie as Mr Rennie? If she did, Simon would know immediately who he was and what she'd contrived. But she'd never in her conversations with Simon referred to Bertie by that name, so it would probably be best just to introduce him as such.

Where the hell had they got to? Conversation with Bertie was becoming stilted; all he wanted to talk about was her writing, and she was unable to concentrate sufficiently to give meaningful responses to his observations. She'd tried holding his hand, but he'd withdrawn his on first contact.

What the hell. She didn't actually fancy him; if she needed a really good seeing to, he'd be the last person she'd choose.

The doorbell rang. At last! She stood up and pulled down her skirt. She'd deliberately chosen a knee-length one. Although her legs were good, they couldn't compete with bloody Jessica's. She hadn't wanted Bertie to make comparisons.

'That'll be Simon and Jessica. I'll let them in. Oh, there's no need to get up, Bertie. We don't stand on ceremony.'

This is it then. She went to the front door and opened it.

'Hello, you two! Come on in. Just one thing before you go into the lounge.' She lowered her voice. 'I have a guest who'll be joining us for dinner. A gentleman friend.'

She noticed the glance that Simon and Jessica exchanged when she said that, and the grin that came to Jessica's face, damn her.

She led them into the lounge. Despite what she had told him, Bertie was standing up.

'This is my friend Bertie,' she said, 'and Bertie, this is my son Simon and his partner, Jessica.' On saying this, she immediately took up a position from where she could observe all three of them. Bertie shook both their hands. There was no indication from his expression that he recognised Jessica, but then she would have been only 16 when he last saw her, wouldn't she?

But as soon as Bertie released her hand, Jessica stepped back, a puzzled expression on her face which changed to a wide-eyed stare, then to one of horrified amazement. She took another two steps back, stumbling against the arm of a chair.

Stephanie turned to look at Bertie. He seemed composed, but this lasted only a few seconds. He then shook his head from side to side, his mouth open, his eyes blinking.

'Jane', he said in a voice that trembled. 'Oh, my God. Jane. Jane.' He clasped his forehead, peering at Jessica from under his hand.

For a brief moment, nobody moved. Then there was an outraged bellow from Simon. 'You bastard! You're that Rennie fellow, aren't you?'

'And you cow!' he shouted at Stephanie. 'How long have you both been planning this? And what for, for Christ's sake? Thought you'd get a kick out of it, did you? You're a couple of perverts!'

He turned to Jessica, who was now leaning against the arm of the chair, but her face was now devoid of any expression. 'Come on, darling, let's go home and leave these depraved old saddos to their own devices.'

Then Bertie stepped towards him.

'Simon,' he said. 'Listen. You've got this all wrong. I didn't know anything about this. It was your mother who – '

Simon turned, raised his arm, and punched Bertie hard in the face. He fell backwards, and his head banged against the occasional table. He collapsed on the floor, his eyes closed. Stephanie screamed when the first blow landed and again when his head hit the table. She bent over him.

'Bertie! Bertie! Are you all right?' She turned to look up at Simon. 'He's unconscious! What have you done? You call yourself a doctor?'

Simon peered down at Bertie. 'His eyes are opening. He'll probably recover soon. If he doesn't, call an ambulance. Anyway, I'm sure you'll look after him in your own inimitable way.' He stood up. 'Come on, Jess, let's go.'

He took her arm and led her out.

Stephanie was left kneeling over Bertie, who'd begun to moan. She hadn't anticipated the afternoon ending this way, but it gave her inspiration for an even better climax to her novel.

Chapter 31

Jessica was silent on the drive home and sat motionless beside him. How Simon wished he could hold her hand. All he could do was keep repeating, 'I'll be all right Jess,' but he knew this was an absurd statement. How could things ever be right again? The past which he thought she'd successfully buried had loomed up, probably to overwhelm her. And one thing was certain, she'd never want to see his mother again. He didn't think he did, either.

He kept his arm round her as they walked from the car to the house. Once inside, he settled her onto the settee.

'Is there anything I can get you, darling?'

She shook her head. He sat down beside her and took her hand. He had not the slightest idea what to say to her. Then she turned to him.

'Si, do you think Dad's been seriously hurt?'

Simon was taken aback, amazed that she could call that Rennie fellow 'dad' and that she should express concern about his injuries.

'I think it was only mild concussion, Jess. And he deserved everything he got.'

'But didn't you hear what he said? He said he knew nothing about what was going on. It wasn't him who planned it.'

'I don't believe that, Jess. He's been in contact with Mum for ages. He must have been party to it.'

'I'm not so sure.'

'But Jess, even if that's so, it must have been horrible to be confronted with him after all these years.'

She fell silent, then, 'I think I'd like a cup of tea. Could you make me one?'

'Of course.'

When he returned to her with the tea, she was sitting upright, looking more alert.

'Si, I'd like you to phone your mother, just to check that Dad's okay.'

'What? Why are you so concerned about him? He and your mother abused you, didn't they? Forced you to leave home, change your name so they couldn't contact you.'

She took a sip of tea.

'Sit down, Si. I've never spoken much about it to you, have I? Now that I've seen Dad, I'd like to tell you everything that happened.'

'Well, if you're sure it won't upset you.'

'I want to get it all off my chest. I've been trying to forget it for years. Most of the time I can, but then it all comes back to me. That's why I get depressed sometimes.'

Simon clasped her hand. 'Well, if you're sure.'

'I am. Look, my mother was a religious nut-case. I don't know what sort of religion she had, she never explained to me. But she used to slap me whenever I was the slightest bit naughty. Even when I was a young child, I can remember her saying, "You'll not grow up in sin like I have," while she was hitting me.'

'Why didn't your father try to stop her?'

'He wasn't around much when I was a kid. When he wasn't at work, he spent most of his time up in his study. He didn't talk to me much. I suppose he couldn't relate to a young child. I thought all fathers were like that. Anyway, the spankings got worse when I was at primary school because my mother was a teaching assistant at the school and got to hear if I misbehaved.'

'In what way worse?'

'She started using a strap. On my bare bottom.'

'Oh, Jess, you poor kid'.

'I thought when I went to secondary school things would get better, but they didn't, especially when I reached adolescence. She punished me if she caught me listening to pop music, and if my skirt was too short, or if I swore – she called it blaspheming. That's when she started using a cane.'

'On your bare …'

'Yes.'

'But … but why didn't you fight her off? Or tell someone at school?'

'I was terrified of her. I'd been in thrall to her since I was a baby, I suppose.'

'And your father still didn't intervene?'

'Si, I'm finding this difficult. Please hear me out. One evening, I think I was 15, she gave a terrible beating. Can't remember what I'd done. I went to my bedroom, bawling my eyes out. Then … then Dad came in. He didn't say anything, he just cuddled me until I stopped crying.'

She took another sip of tea.

'Then, that started happening a lot, whenever he knew I'd been punished. Sometimes I was in bed, and … and he got on the bed and cuddled me.'

'Christ almighty.'

'No, it's not what you're thinking. But … well, I suppose it was because I was an adolescent, but I started having peculiar feelings when he cuddled me. I didn't know what they were, not then. But I do now. And Si – I enjoyed it.'

'But did he touch you inappropriately?'

'No, I don't think so. But I was an innocent as far as sex was concerned, even though my schoolmates seemed to talk about nothing else.'

'Jess, I need a stiff drink. D'you want one?'

'No, I'm okay.'

She seemed to be. Simon was amazed that she was being so calm because he wasn't. He poured himself a large scotch and re-joined her on the settee.

'Nearly finished now. In the Sixth Form, I got quite friendly with Phoebe, a girl in my class. I started telling her what was going on at home. One day, I started crying when I was telling her. The next day, she told me she'd told her parents what I was going through, and they'd suggested I leave home and move in with them.'

'Good for them.'

'Yes, well, I started thinking about it. Then, after one particularly vicious beating, I decided to do it. I told Dad.

He didn't say much, he never did, but he helped me pack when my mother was out and ordered a taxi so I could leave without seeing her.'

'Did you ever see either of them again?'

'No. Dad tried to call on me once, but Phoebe's mother refused to let him in.'

'I don't blame her.'

'But the thing was, Phoebe hadn't just told her parents about the beatings. She told them about Dad cuddling me in bed. They told me that was sexual abuse. They wanted to tell the police, but I wouldn't let them. But what they said made me start to wonder if Dad *had* abused me. I was so naïve. But by that time, I'd been accepted at university, so I decided I never wanted to see my parents again and to change my name when I got to uni.'

'Oh, Jess, darling, why did you never tell me all this before?'

'Because by the time I met you, I thought I'd put it all behind me. When I got to uni, things started to change for me. Okay, my first year was a bit dismal, but after that, I started making friends and doing all the things that students do. One friend told me I was attractive and showed me what to wear, how to do my hair and wear make-up. Most of the time, I was able to forget about my parents, though I suppose they were there in the back of my mind. Then I really got into the swing of things, went to raves, got chatted up by the boys. Then ... well, I started putting it about. I think I've told you about that.'

'Yes, you have. You were very frank about that part of your past.'

'Then after I graduated, I got a job as a pharmacist here in Leeds, and I met you. The rest you know.'

As she spoke the final sentences, her voice began to quaver. Simon turned to face her. Tears had begun pouring down her cheeks. He pulled her towards him. She put her head on his shoulder and burst into sobs.

'Darling, what's the matter? Is it something to do with meeting me?'

'No, of course not.' The sobs continued. All Simon could do was to hold her. Minutes passed before the sobs began to subside into sniffles, then she was silent. Simon looked at her, and she was smiling.

'Jess, what's amusing you?'

'Nothing. I just feel so relieved. Relieved that I've told you everything. It's the first time I've ever done that. And now I've seen my dad again, I want to tell him everything's all right.'

'Are you sure about that? Wouldn't it be better to let sleeping dogs lie?'

She kissed him. 'Si, you've been wonderful. Don't know what I'd do without you. But I must see Dad again. You do understand that, don't you?'

'Well, if you say so.'

'So, could you call your mother and ask her if Dad's okay? Then say if he is, that I want to see him before he leaves to go home. It's not too late to phone now, is it?'

'Jess, the last thing I want to do now is to speak to my bloody mother.'

'I'll do it then.' She jumped to her feet. 'What's your mother's number?'

Simon had no alternative but to tell her and then to sit listening to her end of the conversation.

- 'Mrs Bridges? It's Jessica here, though you probably know by now I was once called Jane Johnson …'

- 'No, listen to me, will you. First of all, is my dad all right?'

- 'Well, I think if Simon had known the whole story, it might not have been my dad he'd have hit. No, listen, please. There's something else I want to say. I want to see Dad tomorrow, assuming he wants to see me, and …'

- 'No, Mrs Bridges. I don't ever want to enter your house again. Tell my dad that Simon will arrive at your place at nine o'clock tomorrow to pick him up and bring him over here. Ask him to be ready at the door.'

- 'Good.'

She replaced the receiver. 'She says Dad's okay. And I think he'll agree to come over here. You don't mind, do you?

'Not if that's what you want. Jess, I'm amazed. I've never seen you so assertive. Don't tell me what my mother said. I don't want to know.'

She sat down next to him of the settee, a grin on her face.

'I feel even better for that. It's been quite a day, hasn't it? I think we deserve an early night.'

She kissed him on the lips. It was a long kiss.

Chapter 32

As he drove towards his mother's house, Simon was apprehensive and still filled with uncertainty. He couldn't be sure that his mother would comply with Jess's request and ask Rennie – or Johnson was it now? – to stand by the door, ready to be collected. The last thing he wanted was to be confronted with his mother.

And what about Johnson? Would the man even want to get in the car, given that his last contact with Simon had been a fist in his face? Simon had tried to persuade Jess to come with him, but she'd said she didn't want to risk meeting his mother, and in any case, she'd resolved never to go near her house again.

Not only was he apprehensive but plagued with guilt. He'd never assaulted anyone before, never even considered it. He was a doctor, for God's sake, supposedly a pillar of the community. What if Johnson decided to press charges? That might mean the end of his career. The first thing he must do when Johnson got in the car, always assuming he'd do so, would be to apologise.

He drew up outside the house. There was no one standing outside. He sat for a minute, steeling himself to go to the front door. He couldn't do it. So he blasted the car horn. No result. He blasted it again, keeping his hand on the button.

The front door opened, and Johnson stepped out. No sign of Mother, thank Christ. Simon got out of the car and beckoned to him. As he approached, Simon noticed a cut on his temple and the beginnings of bruising on his cheek.

He opened the passenger door. 'Good morning, Mr. Bridges,' Johnson said as he stepped in.

'Good morning,' Simon replied, still unsure how he should address him. He got in the car and drove away. There were several minutes of uncomfortable silence.

'Thank you for giving me the opportunity to see my daughter again, Mr Bridges.'

'That's quite alright Mr … look, I'm not sure how I should address you.'

'My name's Johnson, but please call me Jeremy.'

Simon wasn't sure he was ready for such familiarity but responded by telling him to call him Simon. Silence fell again.

'Mr John … Jeremy, I must apologise for hitting you last night. I didn't hear you say that you weren't party to planning that outrageous scenario. You must understand I was angry on behalf of Jess. But, in any case, what I did was unforgivable, and me a doctor.'

'I'm a doctor as well.'

'Really? Jess didn't tell me that. I thought you were some sort of writer.'

'I have a Ph.D. in English Literature. And my daughter's name is Jane.'

There was no answer to that. Simon decided to keep his counsel until they got home.

'Jess! We're home! Come in, Jeremy.'

Simon ushered him into the lounge. Jess was in there, standing in the middle of the room.

'Dad. Oh, Dad!'

'Jane. My dear Jane.'

They stepped towards each other, hesitantly at first, then Jeremy held his arms open. She ran to him, and he flung his arms round her. Simon heard her start to weep.

'You two have got a lot of catching up to do,' he said. 'I'll leave you to it. I'll get some lunch. Let me know when you're ready to join me.'

Neither of them answered. They were still standing, holding each other. Simon left them to it. As he entered the kitchen, he was wondering what the future would now hold, and whether Jess would still be the same woman he'd come to adore. Of one thing he was certain, he would never, ever, call her Jane.

WINTER

Chapter 33

There was only a fortnight to go before the shortest day. Jeremy was sitting in his subtly-lit kitchen eating the roast beef dinner prepared for him by Mrs Hobbes, the woman he now called his housekeeper, and gazing round to look with satisfaction at the modern equipment – oven and hob, dishwasher, washing machine, fridge-freezer – installed a few weeks previously. He preferred to eat in the kitchen rather than the dining room which had yet to be re-carpeted and re-furnished, a job which was due to start in the new year.

He had been fortunate in his choice of a cleaner, a motherly old soul who'd started by visiting only once a week, but who'd been happy to extend her duties to include shopping, then later to washing and ironing, and ultimately to cooking him an evening meal on Mondays, Wednesdays, and Fridays, though she'd said her husband would object if she were to provide that service at the weekends.

He finished his dinner – it was excellent as always – and loaded the dishwasher, having decided against eating the apple pie prepared by Mrs Hobbes. He was starting to put on more weight, and all the new clothes he'd purchased were beginning to feel tight, especially the brown sports jacket, dark grey flannel trousers and Viyella shirts which Alisa had said particularly suited him. He brewed coffee in the cafetiere and carried the cup into the lounge. It was time for the six o'clock news. He turned on the 40-inch television and sank back into the plush armchair, only briefly regretting that there was no-one present with whom he could sit on the equally luxurious settee.

His viewing was interrupted by the phone ringing. He muted the television and looked at the handset read-out, easy to decipher through his new varifocals – oh no, it was Rosemary. What the hell did she want?

'Hello, Rosemary.'

'Jeremy, sorry to disturb you at this time in the evening. Would it be all right if I paid you a quick visit?'

'Well, I'm rather busy at the moment. Can't you tell me what this is about?'

'No, I'd prefer to say what I have to say face to face. I won't keep you long. I can be with you in ten minutes.'

'Oh, very well, if you must.' He pressed the off switch.

Damn the woman. Recently, she'd been pestering him with phone calls, asking him when he was going over to see Helen, telling him she was getting much better and how she'd probably like to see him. Probably? That hardly indicated enthusiasm on Helen's part. She'd gone to live with Rosemary, not that she'd ever made that intention explicit. She'd begun by just spending increasing amounts of time over there, and he'd noticed that she'd begun taking her personal possessions with her and not bringing them back. Then a whole week had passed when she'd slept there, and since the start of November, she hadn't returned home, if home was how she still thought of his house. He wasn't upset about this, just mildly offended, and her absence meant that he felt under no obligation to tell her about his change of fortune.

He could no longer concentrate on the news – it was always depressing anyway – and he turned the television off. But he must remember to record tonight's BBC 4 programme about the birth of British blues music, which Jim Ellison had urged him to watch. He didn't want to watch it live because late evening was when he felt most inspired to write. And the advantage of recording the programme was that he could zap through it if it were not to his taste, which he doubted it would be. But he didn't want to offend Jim, whom he now met regularly in the *Bricklayers Arms* and whose house he'd visited on several occasions to join him and his wife for dinner. He was getting to like Jim because he no longer mocked or teased him and was happy to talk about literature, though he still evidently had a mission to try to educate him about popular culture. And he'd never once mentioned Helen's conviction.

The doorbell rang. He let Rosemary in and took her into the lounge, noticing her wide-eyed amazement at its transformation.

'Good heavens, Jeremy, I hardly recognise this room. It must have cost you a fortune. Have you told Helen what you've had done?'

'No, but no doubt you will.' He didn't invite her to sit down, but after taking off her overcoat, she perched on the edge of the settee. Jeremy chose to remain standing.

'So, what is it you've come to tell me that couldn't be said on the phone?'

'Just two things. Firstly, are you aware how much better Helen is now she's begun to question her religious beliefs?'

'No. We never contact each other as well you know.'

'Well, perhaps when you hear this, you might feel able to see her. Look, Jeremy, I'm an agnostic. But I've told her that I was raised to believe in a merciful God, one who would always forgive someone who repented his or her sins. We talk about this almost every evening, and at last, I'm getting through to her. I think the turning point came when I told her that if she believed she committed a mortal sin by having sex before marriage, then surely you had as well? And if that was the case, why was God not punishing you in the same way He was punishing her?'

'To which her reply was?'

'She didn't reply. But ever since then, I've noticed a gradual lightening of her mood. Last week she asked me if I thought that God might have forgiven her for hitting Leroy Mylie. I said, of course He had. She's started smiling, Jeremy, and even laughing, once at a rather risqué joke on a TV programme, though I'm not sure she understood it.'

'Why are you telling me all this?'

'Because I think you need to know. And wouldn't you feel better if you spoke to her again, so the two of you could come to some sort of accommodation?'

'Possibly. So long as she won't think that accommodation will lead to co-habitation.'

'I don't think you need worry about that.'

'Well, I'll think about it. What was the second thing you wanted to say?'

'Look, I realise it might be difficult for you to think of a reason to come round and see her after all this time. So, I'm going to give you a reason. Jeremy, I'm inviting you to come and join us at Christmas, just for dinner if you'd prefer, but you'd be welcome to come early and spend the whole day with us.'

Jeremy was taken aback. Christmas had always been a dismal time for him ever since his mother had died. First, with his father, each searching for things to talk about over a dinner of sausage and mash, then, with Helen who refused to celebrate the season on the grounds that the pagan winter solstice celebrations were forbidden to true believers. But this year, he had something to look forward to, and it certainly wouldn't be a yuletide spent with Helen.

'Thank you for the offer, Rosemary, but I have other plans for Christmas day.'

'Really?' Rosemary's astonishment was palpable.

'Yes. Now, if that's all you came to say, I have some work that – '

He wasn't allowed to finish the sentence. Rosemary rose, struggled into her overcoat, and marched out of the room. When Jeremy opened the front door for her, she didn't bid him goodbye and walked straight to her car.

In the past, Jeremy would have been affronted by such a display of bad manners, assuming it to be evidence of the miscreant's lack of education, but now such behaviour resulted in only a metaphorical shrugging of his shoulders. He had better things to think about. His study was beckoning to him. But first, he had to set up the TV to record that bloody programme. That having been done, he decided to get on with trying to write his new novel.

It was a total pleasure to enter his study, for it was now solely a room in which to engage in the creative process rather than it having to double-up as a place of refuge. The study was the first room in the house to have benefitted from Eustace's largesse. It had filing cabinets, purpose-built shelving, a comfortable office chair, a desk specifically designed to accommodate his new computer and keyboard, and a printer. On the wall above the desk were three photographs: the one of Eustace taken when he was a young soldier, one of Jane taken at his last visit to her, and one of Alisa which she'd given him when he'd asked for one.

He sat down at the computer but found he was unable to start working because the conversation he'd had with Rosemary had brought to mind a dilemma with which he was faced. Hers was the third invitation for him to join people for Christmas, and he'd discounted that. But the other two invitations were from Jane and Alisa, and he couldn't decide which one to accept.

He had paid several visits to Jane and Simon since that fateful day two months ago. He always left feeling slightly disappointed. Jane obviously loved seeing him, always embraced and kissed him when he arrived, but he sometimes felt it was like being with a mere acquaintance because she was not the child he remembered, but a young professional woman whose life he knew little about. After she'd told him that there was no way she wanted Helen to know that he'd found her, they agreed not to talk further about their shared past. But this made it hard to relate to the confident, almost assertive person she'd grown into. She was a scientist with no interest in literature or the arts, so they had little in common. But she was his daughter, and he loved her.

As for Simon, Jeremy's initial reservations about him had diminished after conversations with him alone in the *Original Oak*. They'd spoken about Stephanie only once.

Apparently, Simon and his mother had agreed to an armistice, though it would be some time before a peace treaty could be signed. She'd given up the idea of writing a novel after meeting a new man-friend. Jeremy's growing affinity with Simon resulted from his medical expertise. He'd confided in him about his incontinence problem and was told to seek a diagnosis immediately. He'd undergone tests at the private hospital in Watford and had dreaded hearing the result, fearing the worse, but it transpired it was benign prostate enlargement which could be, and indeed had been, alleviated by taking medicine.

It was Simon who had raised the issue of Jeremy's red-blotched nose. 'It's rosacea,' he'd told him. 'Easily cured by Rozex ointment. Get your GP to prescribe it.' Jeremy had, and the embarrassment he'd suffered since being a teenager vanished almost overnight.

But Jeremy was never disappointed after a day spent with Alisa, whom he'd visited five times since Eustace's funeral. He thoroughly enjoyed her company and discovering more about her. She had no interest in literature, but she surprised him by being highly knowledgeable about the countryside and its history. She took him for walks in the Chilterns and explained how the landscape had evolved. He was overwhelmed by the beauty of the beechwoods in autumn. Perhaps also as a result of his new spectacles, the countryside was no longer a fuzzy, irrelevant backdrop to whatever was in his mind, but something inspirational in which he could immerse himself, and he resolved to describe landscapes in his new novel. His affection for Alisa grew, and she made it clear that this was reciprocated. But it was an affection devoid of any sexual undertones; it was almost as though they were siblings. He found himself missing her whenever they weren't together.

How could he solve the conundrum of whom to visit at Christmas? Maybe one of them would be content with a visit on New Year's Eve? But which one? Christmas was traditionally a family occasion, so he supposed he ought to spend it with Jane and Simon. And yes, on New Year's Eve they'd no doubt want to spend getting drunk with friends of their own age. He was sure that Alisa would understand that he'd need to visit Jane over Christmas, and she might welcome him coming the following week. He decided to phone her now to ask her.

'Hello, Alisa?'

'Hello, Jeremy, I was just thinking about you.'

'Alisa, about your invitation to join you for Christmas. I'd love to come, but I think I'm duty bound to spend it with Jane. I'm so sorry. I'd much prefer to spend it with you.'

'Oh, I quite understand, Jeremy. Family has to come first. I was feeling a bit guilty about not going over to my son's, so I'll do that instead.'

'I was wondering, Alisa, how would you feel about me coming over for New Year's Day?'

'Snap! I was thinking just the same thing. Come over on New Year's Eve, then we can see the New Year in together.'

'Great! I'll do that.'

The remainder of their conversation was taken up by them recounting what each had been doing over the past few days. It was only after he'd turned off the phone that it hit Jeremy: if they were going to see in the New Year in together, it would mean he'd be staying with her overnight. That would, he was sure, add to the pleasure of his stay. And of one thing he was certain, it would be a chaste visit.

At ease with himself, he decided to give attention to his novel.

Chapter 34

A host of ideas for the novel had been jostling for position in his mind for nearly two months, and he'd been making notes on them but had not reached the stage of committing them to manuscript form, until tonight. Reluctant as he had been to admit it, Stephanie's avowed intention to write a novel based on family relationships held a certain appeal now that he'd been reunited with Jane and had a daughter as well as a wife, if thus she could still be called.

But it was remembering Eustace's shout of 'atonement!' that had provided something approaching inspiration. Eustace had, of course, committed a crime for which he had not been punished, and he'd seen writing an autobiography as a means of achieving some sort of liberation from a lifetime of guilt. Jeremy had committed no crime and had nothing about which to feel guilty – or had he? No, he felt no guilt, but he had begun to have regrets.

His biggest regret was, of course, not having tried to protect Jane from her mother's assaults. He'd convinced himself that child-raising was a wife's responsibility, but he knew now this was not a valid excuse. Which led to the second regret – having spent so much of his life at home cocooned in his study in the belief that his true destiny was to write a literary masterpiece. This, he now realised, had led to social isolation. He'd believed his work colleagues and other casual acquaintances to be unworthy of the attention of an academic who, by rights, should have a Ph.D. in English Literature.

But he couldn't place the blame for his isolation solely on his writing. As a young man, he'd always been uncomfortable in the company of those who had non-academic interests, those who talked about little other than pop music, and football, and sex, and current fashions. So he'd deliberately adopted a persona akin to that found not just amongst those of his father's generation but of his grandfather's. He'd avoided the use of contemporary slang, dressed as though it were the 1940s, read few novels that had been published after 1960, and went to classical music concerts even though he was not in any way musical. He'd deliberately made himself a man apart in order not to be embarrassed by contact with those with whom he had nothing in common.

Of course, he certainly regretted his marriage, but this was something forced on him. Should he feel guilty about not having helped Helen overcome her mental illness, even if only by insisting she sought treatment? But on the rare occasions he'd tried, she'd always responded with a religious diatribe. No, he had no reason to feel guilty.

But now, having developed relationships with Eustace and Alisa, with Jane and Simon, and yes, even with Stephanie, he'd decided that he might find a way of confronting his regrets by writing about contemporary society in a new novel, and it *would* be a novel, not an autobiography. Autobiographies were only successful when written by the famous or by those who had experienced major historical events. He'd considered an autobiographical novel, but the genre was not to his taste.

No. He would write a novel. But this time, he would unashamedly draw on his personal experiences in devising parts of the plot and some of the characters within it. Most novelists probably did this, even though they might be unaware of it. He didn't believe that any novel, even science fiction or horror, was entirely the product of the author's imagination. Even if subconsciously, events in one's past and the people one knew influenced the storylines and characters.

The narrative would not be written in the first person. He knew he would find such a device restrictive. And the third person narrative would not be written from the viewpoint of one character. This he would also find restrictive. He knew that some writers asserted that the characterisation and character development of protagonists should be revealed through their actions and dialogue, but Jeremy believed a reader should also be aware of what the major characters were thinking and feeling. After all, one often did and said things that were totally at variance with what was going on in one's head. So he would give many of his characters a narrative voice and inner monologues. He would make them wonder about things, and ask themselves questions, reveal their hidden worries and uncertainties.

He was ready to commit fingers to the keyboard. He typed the opening paragraph of the first chapter:

Doreen and Eileen, both widowed and in their late 70s, had moved into Barnes Avenue within a few weeks of each other in the 1960s. It had then been part of a council estate, but in common with most other tenants, they had exercised the right bestowed on them by Mrs Thatcher in 1980 to buy their homes a large discount. Many of the houses had now been sold on, and the estate was no longer the close-knit community they remembered.

He was about to continue typing when his telephone rang. The read-out informed him it was Jane calling. Damn. He'd better answer it. She'd probably want to talk about Christmas.

'Hello, Jane.'

'Hi, Dad.'

'Are you phoning about Christmas? I was going to ring you later about that.'

'Never mind about that now. Listen, Dad. There's something I need to tell you. It's been on my mind for ages. I've only just plucked up courage to phone you.'

'What's that, then?'

'I … I think I ought to see Mum.'

'What?'

'I still don't know if it's the right thing to do, but I've got a bit of a conscience about her now that I'm reunited with you. I don't think I can really put the past behind me until I've seen her. Can you tell her that? Do you think she'd want to see me?'

'I … I honestly don't know, Jane.'

'Well, will you ask her? Please, Dad? Dad? Are you still there?'

'Yes, I'm here. I'm just … well, shell-shocked, I suppose.'

'I'm sorry to put this on you. But I need to know.'

'Are you sure you're being wise, Jane? What good can come from it? You might end up being really hurt.'

'I've thought about that, but it's something I have to do. Dad, please say you'll ask her if she'd be willing to see me.'

'Very well. If you insist.'

'Oh, thanks so much! I'd better go now, Dad. I need to tell Simon immediately. See you at Christmas. Bye!'

Jeremy's first thought on putting down the phone wasn't about the things that might arise from a meeting between Jane and Helen. He was thinking about his novel. It was planned to end with a denouement, but now it seemed there was going to be a late climax. This would mean significant re-writing of the final chapters.

His annoyance at this was suddenly tempered by the thought that the unexpected late climax might inspire him to write a follow-up novel.

THE END

Lightning Source UK Ltd.
Milton Keynes UK
UKHW010122070821
388442UK00003B/1085